FAITH HOLDS THE KEY

BY

FRANCINE A. YATES

PUBLISHED BY YATES PUBLISHING LLC
P.O. Box 18982
Indianapolis, Indiana 46218

This is a work of fiction. All events, characters, places and incidents are strictly products of the author's imagination. Any similarities to persons living or dead are completely coincidental.

Scriptures quotations are taken from the King James Version of the Bible.

2nd Edition:

Printed in the United States

ISBN: 978-09778521-1-6

ACKNOWLEDGMENTS

First and foremost, to God be the glory for the many things he has done to bless my life.

To: Etoria Wilson, thank you for your prayers, and words of encouragement.

To: Nadine Hill, thank you for your prayers, and cheering me on to complete this book. You have encouraged me daily, and for that I am grateful.

To: James Patterson, my editor, I couldn't have done this without you.

To: Timothy O. Williams, my graphic artist.

To: all the book clubs throughout the country, and bookstores who have supported me, I thank you for allowing me to be a part of your collection.

And, of course, to all my readers everywhere, thank you for supporting me!

Other Books by Francine A. Yates

CARRIE O AND ME
WHAT A WOMAN GOD MADE

Linda, our heroine, returns to her old neighborhood with mixed haunting emotional feelings of her childhood. She flashes back to the times of being cared for by a loving and God-fearing woman who devoted her life to making the world a better place. Linda is also on a mission to fulfill a promise she made on the deathbed of Mrs. Carrie O. That promise was to make peace with her birth mother, Vivian, and forgive her for the pain she inflicted upon Linda in childhood. Linda's story is one of triumph over adversities and hope over despair. Her deep abiding faith provides the foundation of her success

CHAPTER ONE

While lying in my plaid chaise lounge chair under my matching umbrella taking in the rays of the sun, I can't help but think about the bountiful blessings God has given me. Just a little over three weeks ago, I was in a coma and laid up in the hospital in Jacksonville, Florida. Now, here I am back home in Atlanta and enjoying my home. Life is good! I got a glass of sun-made iced tea and sat on the deck floor along with my bare plate having just devoured two slices of meat-lover's pizza. I smiled to myself thinking about the nice slice of key lime pie I will be eating as soon as my neighbor, Denise, and her niece, Kalahia, return from the neighborhood bakery.

I reached for my Bible to spend some quality time with God until Denise returns. I flipped pages remembering some of the scriptures Mrs. Carrie used to teach me. But no matter how many we read or talked about my feeling, I always came back to the 23rd Psalm: *The Lord is my shepherd; I shall not want. He maketh me to lie down in green pastures: he leadeth me beside the still waters. He restoreth my soul: he leadeth me in the paths of righteousness for his name sake. Yea, though I walk through the valley of the shadow of death, I will fear no evil: for thou art with me; thy rod and thy staff they comfort me. Thou preparest a table before me in the presence of mine enemies: thou anointest my head with oil; my cup runneth over. Surely goodness and mercy shall follow me all the days of my life: and I will dwell in the house of the Lord forever.*

As I read this scripture, I could actually feel the presence of the Lord. God has been my shepherd. He protected me and allowed me to return back to Brandon and my mother. When I think about my close walk with the shadow of death, I could actually feel chill bumps covering my body.

I closed the Bible and whispered a soft prayer, "Lord I thank you for bringing me back to life. I mean, giving me another chance."

So caught up in the word of God; the sound of a phone ringing sparked me back to reality.

Who in the world could be calling me while I am spending some quality time with my God? I sure hope it's not Denise. All she had to do was go a few blocks to the bakery and pick up our pie.

"Hello?"

From the sobs and static on my cordless phone, I couldn't understand what this person was saying and just who it was.

"Hello, if you can't speak any clearer I'm going to hang up this phone; now who is this?"

"Linda, this is mother."

"Mother, why all the crying? What is wrong with you?"

"I have some bad news."

"Mother, has your cancer come back?"

"No, I'm still in remission. Forget about me. It's Paul my God, Paul!"

"What do you mean, it's Paul? Mother, you aren't making sense. Calm down and tell me, what about Paul?"

"He, oh my God, I can't say it, he…he has been accused of fondling one of the young girls at our school.

Now faith is the substance of things hoped for,
the evidence of things not seen.

Hebrews 11:1

To the loving memory of Mrs. Carrie O. Riggins Pettway, my aunt

Benjamin F. Yates, my beloved husband

My devoted children:

Donald L. Harrison Jr.

Patrice A. Fuller

My Parents:

Leonard W. & Ernestine Riggins Burnett

My brother & sisters:

Frank Gossett; Terri Brooks; Valencia Rascoe; Kathi Burnett; Delia Burnett; Lezlie Burnett

Prayer Partners:

Evangelist Walter Rean Moore
Sister Josephine Charleston
Evangelist Doris Hill
Evangelist Carolyn Drane

Rev. Charles W. & Flossie Harris Sr., Pastor
Pleasant Union Missionary Baptist Church
Indianapolis, Indiana

ACKNOWLEDGMENTS

First and foremost, to God be the glory for the many things he has done to bless my life.

To: Etoria Wilson, thank you for your prayers, and words of encouragement.

To: Nadine Hill, thank you for your prayers, and cheering me on to complete this book. You have encouraged me daily, and for that I am grateful.

To: James Patterson, my editor, I couldn't have done this without you.

To: Timothy O. Williams, my graphic artist.

To: all the book clubs throughout the country, and bookstores who have supported me, I thank you for allowing me to be a part of your collection.

And, of course, to all my readers everywhere, thank you for supporting me!

Other Books by Francine A. Yates

CARRIE O AND ME
WHAT A WOMAN GOD MADE

Linda, our heroine, returns to her old neighborhood with mixed haunting emotional feelings of her childhood. She flashes back to the times of being cared for by a loving and God-fearing woman who devoted her life to making the world a better place. Linda is also on a mission to fulfill a promise she made on the deathbed of Mrs. Carrie O. That promise was to make peace with her birth mother, Vivian, and forgive her for the pain she inflicted upon Linda in childhood. Linda's story is one of triumph over adversities and hope over despair. Her deep abiding faith provides the foundation of her success

CHAPTER ONE

While lying in my plaid chaise lounge chair under my matching umbrella taking in the rays of the sun, I can't help but think about the bountiful blessings God has given me. Just a little over three weeks ago, I was in a coma and laid up in the hospital in Jacksonville, Florida. Now, here I am back home in Atlanta and enjoying my home. Life is good! I got a glass of sun-made iced tea and sat on the deck floor along with my bare plate having just devoured two slices of meat-lover's pizza. I smiled to myself thinking about the nice slice of key lime pie I will be eating as soon as my neighbor, Denise, and her niece, Kalahia, return from the neighborhood bakery.

I reached for my Bible to spend some quality time with God until Denise returns. I flipped pages remembering some of the scriptures Mrs. Carrie used to teach me. But no matter how many we read or talked about my feeling, I always came back to the 23rd Psalm: *The Lord is my shepherd; I shall not want. He maketh me to lie down in green pastures: he leadeth me beside the still waters. He restoreth my soul: he leadeth me in the paths of righteousness for his name sake. Yea, though I walk through the valley of the shadow of death, I will fear no evil: for thou art with me; thy rod and thy staff they comfort me. Thou preparest a table before me in the presence of mine enemies: thou anointest my head with oil; my cup runneth over. Surely goodness and mercy shall follow me all the days of my life: and I will dwell in the house of the Lord forever.*

As I read this scripture, I could actually feel the presence of the Lord. God has been my shepherd. He protected me and allowed me to return back to Brandon and my mother. When I think about my close walk with the shadow of death, I could actually feel chill bumps covering my body.

I closed the Bible and whispered a soft prayer, "Lord I thank you for bringing me back to life. I mean, giving me another chance."

So caught up in the word of God; the sound of a phone ringing sparked me back to reality.

Who in the world could be calling me while I am spending some quality time with my God? I sure hope it's not Denise. All she had to do was go a few blocks to the bakery and pick up our pie.

"Hello?"

From the sobs and static on my cordless phone, I couldn't understand what this person was saying and just who it was.

"Hello, if you can't speak any clearer I'm going to hang up this phone; now who is this?"

"Linda, this is mother."

"Mother, why all the crying? What is wrong with you?"

"I have some bad news."

"Mother, has your cancer come back?"

"No, I'm still in remission. Forget about me. It's Paul my God, Paul!"

"What do you mean, it's Paul? Mother, you aren't making sense. Calm down and tell me, what about Paul?"

"He, oh my God, I can't say it, he...he has been accused of fondling one of the young girls at our school.

He has been working after school with the coach and one of the girls at cheerleading practice said Paul cornered her in the girl's locker room and fondled her breast."

"Hold on, mom, do you want me to fly back and be with you?"

"No, you are trying to recuperate yourself. I shouldn't have called and bothered you, but I didn't have anyone to talk to. Honey, you are all I have, if this lie gets out at school, church or in our neighborhood, I will not be able to live. You know how much I love Paul and he would never do anything like this!"

"Mom listen, I will call Brandon and fly down to be with you. God just placed you back into my life and nothing will be able to separate us."

"What about your job?"

"Don't worry I am still on medical leave. I will make a reservation and call you back with the itinerary."

I couldn't hang the phone up fast enough. I knew one day he was going to pay for what he tried to do to me. God don't like ugly! What mom doesn't know is he tried to rape me, so I know that student isn't lying. He just got caught doing wrong. I felt there was more to this story than she was telling. I had to go be a comfort to my mother and find out the truth. I know when my mother gets to the bottom of it she will not be able to accept that her perfect Paul has a problem with young girls.

Denise finally showed up, but she caught me with my head in my hands. I looked up and found her standing in front of me holding the two slices of pie on a tray.

"Linda, the expression on your face! What's the matter? I wasn't gone that long."

"No, Denise. I just got a distressful call from my mother."

"Now you know you can confide in me. I know all about how she has hurt you in the past. Please don't tell me she has severed your relationship already."

"No, hey, where is Kalahia?"

"She decided to stay inside and eat her pie. Something about making a call to one of her friends back home. I told her fifteen minutes and that is long enough."

"Okay, we can talk in private. Sit down and listen. You know I told you when I went home, I found my mother to be a changed woman. She was no longer a drunk, but a Christian lady. Well, she was also married to Paul Richmond. From the time he laid eyes on me, his ways seemed fresh to me."

Denise was about to take a bite of her pie when she placed the folk back on her plate. She sat up and looked right into my eyes and said, "What do you mean seemed fresh to you?"

I sighed, "Well, one day I was in the shower and just as I opened the shower curtain to get out, the bathroom door came flying open. He excused himself after looking me up and down. I took it as a mistake and called it an accident. Mom was out, she went to pick up Brandon to surprise me and I was to be dressed for dinner. I took the time and locked the bathroom door, took a nice, hot shower and before I was able to put on my undergarment, Paul picked the lock and rushed in on me and tried to rape me."

"He did what? Girl, what was Brandon's reaction when you told him about Paul? How did he handle this?"

"I didn't say a word about Paul to Brandon, but when he entered my mother's house and saw the expression on my face, he knew something was wrong. I lied to him. I told him Paul said something out of context to me. To this day, he still doesn't know that Paul tried to rape me."

"Did you tell your mother?"

"No, are you crazy! For the first time since my sister's death, my mother was happy. When she introduced me to Paul, she was laughing, blushing, happy, and just beside herself. I told you she was never married, so Paul was her first and only husband. I asked her how much she knew about this man and she said, grinning from ear to ear, that he had another wife of 18 years, but she died of cancer and that he was by her side until her death. Anyway, I'm going to make some reservations and be there for her."

"Linda, you do what you feel you have to but if I were you, I would fly there to comfort my mother but also I would hire a private investigator and let him do a background check on Mr. Richmond. You don't know what dirt an investigator can dig up. Who knows, his wife might not be dead; just divorced the jerk! Excuse me, but I feel when you go to your mother with what he tried to do to you, you will have written evidence that he has a history of this kind of stuff. Look at me accusing him already. I'm just saying you know what he tried with you and you were there only a few days. He really might actually have a problem and doesn't know it."

"I'm going inside to call the airlines and get on the first plane leaving for Jacksonville, Florida. The next call will be to Brandon. He needs to know what is going on with my mother."

"Yes, you are right. And he needs to know about you and Paul, too."

I threw up both hands to tell her to hold it, but she caught me off guard.

"Don't say a word. Let me finish. You and Brandon are getting married in two months and why go into a marriage keeping secrets."

"Denise, wait, I will take the secret to my grave. I refuse to hurt Brandon or my mother. I have to look at it like this: Paul tried to rape me, but he was unsuccessful. So, why hurt the two people who mean the world to me."

"Linda, you are missing the issue here. All I'm saying is you need to let Brandon know what Paul almost did to you. Like it or not, he did put his hands on you and Brandon, your future husband should know this."

"Denise, I am not listening to you. I refuse to breathe a word about this to my mother or Brandon and if you are truly a friend of mine, you will let it go."

"Okay, but secrets have a way of coming to the surface the minute you try to suppress them. I'm speaking from experience and not just to hear myself talk."

"Denise, please, no stories today. I need to call Brandon, then the airlines to see if I can get a flight out in the next few hours. My mother needs me. I mean, she really needs me."

Denise politely unfolded her napkin, placed it neatly over her pie and said, "Look Linda, I'm here for you; always have been and always will be. I tell you I would hate to be in your shoes and I know you told me no stories, but I will say this. If I were you I would hire Columbo and dig up all the dirt I could on your step-father, Mr. Paul, whoever he is, and I would present it to your mother on a silver platter."

Before I could open my mouth, Denise had made a quick turn and was headed out the back gate. She probably has a point, but I refuse to hurt my mother anymore. She loves Paul and if the accusation is true, then God will open her eyes. I sure don't want to be the one to open them for her. I reached for the phone to call, but not before it started to ring.

"Hello!"

"Linda, hey baby, how are you doing today?"

"Brandon, I was about to call you. My mother has received some terrible news about Paul and she needs me there to comfort her."

"What about Paul, baby. Is he ill, hurt, what?"

"Brandon, I don't know how to tell it to you."

"Just come out with it. Please tell me," he begged, "what's the matter?"

"Mom said Paul was accused of fondling a young girl at the high school."

"Linda, do you believe he is capable of doing such a thing?"

"Brandon I just met him! Why are you asking me a question like that?"

"Linda, I am on my way over. We need to talk."

"Talk," I blurted. "Brandon, it is settled. I'm going to Jacksonville to be with my mother."

"Linda, it isn't about the flight or even about you going. I feel we need to talk about your actions toward Paul, you know before the accident."

"Brandon, I need to call the airline, but please come over and drive me to the airport."

No sooner had I hung up the phone my mind started racing. I was thinking to myself what does he really know? Brandon is a medical doctor, not a psychologist; no way could he know what Paul tried to do to me. I am not going to get myself all worked up over nothing. I felt when Brandon came to Jacksonville after the incident I handled myself like nothing happened.

Chapter Two

I rushed inside to pack a few items of clothing to take with me. With the cordless phone in one hand, I was on the line with Delta making my travel plans. What threw me for a loop was when the lady asked me the date and time of my return flight that I had in mind, I told her one-way ticket please. I had no idea when I was coming back to Atlanta. What seemed like a few minutes must have been hours because the next thing I heard was the doorbell ringing.

"Brandon, you got here in no time."

"It has been a while since we spoke. Did you get your reservation made?"

"Yes, I will be leaving in two hours, but I am only flying one way. I don't know when I will be coming back."

"Linda, I almost lost you in Jacksonville and I don't want to lose you again. What do you mean you don't know when you will be returning?"

"Brandon, my mother needs me and I need to be with her during this crisis. I will be back in a week or two. Remember, I am on sick leave and if I keep feeling this well the doctor will release me soon."

Brandon took me by the waist and held me close. He smells good as always. He looked into my eyes and before I knew it, he was kissing me. All I could do was kiss him back. Lord knows I love this man so much. When I opened my eyes and pushed myself back, Brandon was smiling from ear to ear. He is such a handsome man. I thank God that He placed him in my life.

"Brandon, you take a seat while I finish my packing. I will be ready soon."

Brandon went into the kitchen and I finished my packing. I heard the phone ringing and reached for it, but Brandon had it first. I heard him say something, but I couldn't really make out what he was saying.

"It was Denise and she will get your mail while you are gone."

"Oh! Tell her thanks. No way I can make the post office, have my mail put on hold and still make my flight. She is a great neighbor and friend. She took care of all my mail while I was in Jacksonville before. I was only supposed to be there for a few days which turned into couple weeks."

"Baby, are you sure you want to do this alone?"

"Brandon, you just returned to work and I know you can't go with me. I am all my mother has and I want to be there to support her."

"I know, but I was thinking, does she have any church friends who she can confide in?"

"No, this is too personal and besides I need to be there for her."

"Linda, you are right. I guess I am just looking out for your welfare. Besides, she does need you. Please forgive me for being so selfish."

"Brandon, you aren't being selfish. You are just protecting me. I promise when I rent the car at the airport I will drive slowly and watch out for the other drivers. Honey, you can't be overly protective. I promise I will return in about a week."

Brandon didn't answer. He just reached for my luggage and walked out the front door towards his car. I took a seat on the arm of the sofa and was thinking; do I have everything? Brandon returned like lightening. "Hey, are you sure you're strong enough for this trip?"

"Brandon, I am torn between wanting to be here with you and being with my mother. Forget about my health. I feel great. I just want to be a life support for my mother." I slowly closed the front door as if I wouldn't ever see my condo again.

The drive to the airport was quiet. I'm glad Brandon had the jazz tape playing. I was fresh out of conversation. My mind was really on comforting my mother. I was looking straight ahead, but I could see Brandon out of the corner of my eye. He kept looking in my direction. I know he feels like I'm a little too fragile for the trip, but I can assure him I'm well up to facing Paul Richmond. No sooner than I thought of that name, when the silence was broken, by Brandon.

"Linda, be careful. What if Paul does have a problem with young girls?"

I almost swallowed my tongue. I tried to maintain my composure. "Why Brandon what makes you say such?"

"Like I said, from the time I entered your mother's house, I could feel the friction between you and

Paul, not to mention at dinner when your mother kept asking him if he was alright."

"Lord, help me out of this one," I thought. I took a deep breath and carefully answered, "Brandon, Paul is my step-father and I really don't know him all that well. But, I can assure you that if he has fondled one of those girls, I will make sure he pays dearly for his actions."

I wanted to get Brandon off the subject, so I immediately pointed to the exit ramp for the airport, as if he had never been here before. "Wow! We got here in no time. Linda, I will let you out here. Please don't move. I am going to park and come back and carry your luggage to the Delta counter."

"Brandon, I am not handicapped. I can carry my own luggage."

"Linda, please do as I ask and stay here."

"Okay, Dr. Brandon Alexander, sir."

I watched him drive off and I was about to reach for my luggage when a tall handsome man grabbed my handle and said, "May I help you carry this in?"

"No, my boyfriend is parking the car but thanks anyway."

He smiled showing all his thirty-two pearly white teeth, nodded his head, walked away and disappeared in the crowd. I did as Brandon instructed me to do. Patiently, I waited for his return. It had to be 102 degrees in the shade and every time the glass sliding doors would separate, a gust of cold air rushed to my rescue. Finally, I could see Brandon walking fast towards me. As he approached me, his expression went from serious to friendly. He smiled at me to let me know that everything was either alright or that he was proud that I was still standing in the same spot waiting for his return.

"Hey, let's go in and get your ticket so the sooner you get there the sooner you can return to me. Don't forget we've got a wedding in a few months."

"Brandon, how can I forget in a few months I will be Mrs. Brandon Alexander."

We made our way to the counter and I purchased my ticket, checked my luggage and we strode off to the coffee shop for a bottle of water. Brandon was quiet and so was I. Finally, he broke his silence. Out of nowhere he placed his hands over mine and said, "Linda, if things get out of hand there and emotions get to flying high, I want you to promise me, you won't stay and get stressed out. You will just call it quits and come home. I believe your mother can take her problems to her minister and he can pray and see her through this. Now, I don't want to sound heartless but I am only thinking of your welfare."

Before he could continue, I placed my finger over his lips so he couldn't say another word. "Brandon, I know you think I'm so fragile because of the accident, but I can assure you I'm strong and even stronger in the Lord. If things don't go as I'm hoping, I know how to cut my losses and come back home." Brandon shook his head up and down as if he was agreeing with me. I politely moved my finger. He placed both hands on my face and kissed me on the forehead and smiled. What seemed like minutes went into an hour. My thoughts were infringed by the flight attendant on the microphone barking out which seats were to be boarded first. My seat was 4A so I still had a few minutes to spend with Brandon, since they were boarding the plane from the back first.

"Brandon, they are calling my seat."

"I know and, again, if you need me just call."

He kissed me lightly on the lips. I pulled away and slowly boarded the plane. I turned to look back and he was still standing there looking as if he had tears in his eyes. I could feel my own eyes welling up. I took a deep breath and headed for the plane.

Chapter Three

The pilot and the crew made the trip as pleasant as possible, in spite of the screaming child behind me. The mother was young and all she kept telling the little girl was "shut-up." I personally felt like taking the child to the bathroom and giving her a much-needed spanking. When I first got on the plane and saw her, I thought she was a beautiful little red-headed girl. She was playing with her brother as her mother sat between them. Somewhere between takeoff and landing, she got out of hand. The brother, who looked to be about seven or eight years old, was laughing loudly. The little girl looked to be about three. They were both old enough to know how to sit and conduct themselves in public. When I got off that plane, my head was spinning like I had been on a rough roller coaster ride at Disney World.

I went to retrieve my luggage and from there to the Avis car rental. As I was getting closer to the Avis sign, I started to feel a little dizzy. I focused on the bench and went to take a seat and wait to calm down. I was speaking to my inner self. "Linda, what has gotten into you? I know you aren't afraid to face Paul."

Sweat started popping up on my forehead and I found myself getting short of breath. I opened my mouth to inhale deeply and exhale slowly. This exercise seemed to be helping. I'm beginning to feel normal. While wiping the sweat off my brow, I noticed I was within three feet of the ladies restroom. I slowly made it there. But, not before taking a drink of cold water at the water fountain outside the entrance of the ladies room.

Holding wet paper towels on my forehead for what seemed like hours made a big difference to me. When I first went into the restroom, I felt like I was walking on shaky, weak legs. Now, after leaning on the counter and spending a little time in prayer, I feel like I can make it. I walked back into the airport terminal feeling like my old self. My weak legs had become stronger and I had the attitude of "greater is he that is within me than he that is in the world."

I was walking tall when I made eye contact with the lady at the Avis desk. She smiled at me and I flashed one back to her. "May I help you today?"

"Yes, my name is Linda Smith, and I have a reservation for a mid-size car."

After the paperwork was completed, she must have seen some tiredness in my eyes because as I exited the terminal, I notice she gave me the car that was parked closest to the door. I don't think I could have walked much farther.

I was thinking to myself here I go again back in Jacksonville and under the wheel of a car, where I hadn't been since the accident here that put me into a coma. I knew in my heart that God would protect me. I started the car with mighty confidence and slowly made my way to the interstate.

I pulled the car in front of mom's house, not really knowing what to say or how to act. I sat there for a little while, bowed my head for a short word of silent prayer. I looked up and Paul was coming out of the house. "Linda, may I help you with your bags."

"No, Paul, you look like you are going somewhere so go on. I will get my bags later. I want to be with my mother, but thanks." As I walked into the house, I felt like his eyes were all over me but I couldn't allow my imagination to run wild. I knew I was there for one purpose and that was my mother. In reality, I know what Paul tried to do to me and I believe he tried it with that high school girl, but the problem is convincing my mother.

I walked up to the door and pushed it open and found my mother lying on the sofa in the living room with her eyes closed. "Mother, I'm here for you." She turned and looked at me as if she was either drunk or drugged. She started to wipe her eyes and she looked again like she was trying to focus on me. I walked closer and knelt down by her side. She placed her hand on my face and the tears started to flow. I found my eyes welling up with tears, too.

"Mother, I'm here for you. Please don't cry. God will work it out for you."

With a soft whisper she said, "I know and most of all I am so happy you came to my rescue."

"Mother, I couldn't stay away and let you face this terrible ordeal alone."

"Have you eaten anything, mother?"

"No, I have no appetite but I can make dinner for you."

"No, I will go out and get three dinners and you will eat something."

I went back to the car and made my way across town for three home cooked dinners. I knew my mother had to be hungry and I knew just what would make her want to eat. I pulled up to Jones BBQ and placed an order for two slabs of BBQ ribs with mild sauce, and a large family container of baked beans, potato salad, and a whole chess pie. I loved old man Jones' BBQ with his special sauce. Just the thought of his BBQ made me suck my lips as I pulled up to the next window for pick-up.

Tap, I almost pushed on the gas paddle when I heard the tap on the passenger side of the window! I looked and it was Roy. "Roy, get in and give me a hug. After all, you are the one who went to my mother's house to give her the news about my car accident. What are you doing at the BBQ restaurant? Who's minding the service station?"

"Hey, one question at a time. I have some help and I get to leave for a dinner run for us. Business is still doing good and about your accident, you are welcome. I see you have healed well".

"Yes, God is good and worthy to be praised."

"What brings you back to town so fast?"

"Some personal business with my mother, but I don't intend to stay long. I still have to work on my wedding plans. You do know I am getting married in two months?"

"Yes, remember, you took my address at the service station and said I would get an invitation."

"You are still invited. Wait Roy, let me get my dinners. Before you get out, I want another hug. Again Roy, it was a pleasure seeing you."

"Now, you take your time and make it back to your mothers and I will be looking for that invitation."

"Bye Roy." I slowly pulled off of the lot on to the street and made it in the direction of my mother's house.

My mind ran back to my mother's demeanor when I first came home. She looked as if she was either drugged or she had been drinking, but I didn't smell any alcohol on her breath.

I pulled up and noticed Paul was back so I parked behind his car. I pushed the door open and walked in with the bags full of dinner. Mother was still on the sofa and Paul was nowhere in sight. I placed the bag on the kitchen counter and went back to get my luggage out of the car. When I returned, mother had gotten up and was in the bathroom. I placed my luggage in my room and went into the kitchen to wash my hands and set the table for dinner. Mother finally came out of the bathroom. She really didn't look well at all, but I acted as if I didn't notice how worn out she looked. I placed the BBQ on a large platter and put the side dishes in serving bowls. I set the table for three and called Paul to the table. Mother was already sitting in her favorite seat.

"Look, Mom, BBQ from Mr. Jones. Now I know you want some."

Mom put on a half smile and said, "Yes, I will try and eat a little bit."

Paul came to the table quiet as a church mouse. He looked as if he really has been caught with his hands in the cookie jar. He said, "Linda, thanks for dinner."

"Oh, it was nothing. I knew mother didn't feel like cooking and I know you both needed to eat. I am here to take care of things now." I wanted to say to take care of my mother and not you, but when Mrs. Carrie was alive she said to treat your enemy right, and it would be like heaping coals on his head.

We ate in silence. Mother didn't utter a word and neither did Paul. I did the same and ate in silence, too. My mind was really on trying to find out who this young lady was and get to the bottom of this mess. I was thinking, this is July and I know most of the teachers aren't teaching this summer, but I think if I make a visit to the school, I just might run into someone I knew from the past. I needed a plan and I needed to do this alone. My mother would kill me if she knew that I was investigating this accusation against Paul.

I wish Mrs. Carrie was here. I need someone to talk too, if only I could trust Mrs. Williams or Mrs. Evyonne, but I can't. Those two would spread the news that I didn't trust my stepfather and that I was snooping around the school for answers. I looked over at my mother. She was taking small bites of food. She looked up at me and I put on a wide-mouth smile just so she wouldn't know I was over here plotting on her dear Paul.

After dinner I cleaned up the table and mother was grateful for the dinner. She really didn't have an appetite, but she did manage to eat two bones of ribs and a very small amount of the sides. She loved chess pie, but refused to eat any. All she wanted to do was call it a night. I didn't pressure her. I went into my room to call Monica. I knew she could keep a secret and she liked playing private eye anyway.

"Monica, this is me, Linda. How are you?"

"Linda, hey girl, what's going on?"

"More than I care to talk about on the phone. Hey, can I come and pick you up so we can talk."

"Linda, you mean you are here in Jacksonville! How long have you been here? How long you are staying?"

"Monica, please be quiet. I'm on my way and I will explain everything so be ready. I will pull up in the front of your house in ten minutes so be outside."

I hung up the phone and went into my mother's room to tell her the plans for the evening. When I told her I was spending the night with Monica, her entire expression changed so I cancelled the overnight plans. She gave me her door keys and I headed out to meet Monica.

Chapter Four

Ten minutes later, I was pulling up in front of Monica's house. She was just as eager to see me as I was her. She was jumping up and down. I parked the car and rushed to her for my long awaited hug.

"Linda, it is so good seeing you, girl! You look good. You can't even tell you were in such bad physical shape a few weeks ago."

"Monica, God has healed me completely and I owe it all to Him. Hey, don't forget, we girls have to get together soon for our fittings. You are still going to be my maid-of-honor, aren't you?"

"Linda, don't start any mess. I am the closest thing to a sister you will have. Now stop it. You just say the word and I will be in Atlanta for the fitting. Now, what's all this not talking on the phone about? Please don't tell me you and your mother aren't getting along or is she drinking again?"

"No, get in the car. Let's take a drive and park at the beach. We can talk there."

The drive was all about Monica telling me about her life and what she has been up to while I was in Atlanta and some news about some of our classmates. I was listening and thinking about my mother's situation, too. We finally arrived at the beach, but first we drove through McDonald's for two large strawberry shakes. I parked and looked over at Monica.

"Now Monica, you know I can tell you anything and it won't go any further, can't I?"

"Linda, we have been the best of friends. Of course, you can tell me anything. I have to say you have piqued my interest. You drove me all the way to the beach to talk. We could have stayed at my house to do that."

"No, I wanted to listen to the waves. It seems to calm me down because what I am about to tell you just makes my blood boil when I think about it."

"Don't think - just spit it out. Tell me what's on your mind and what brought you back here so fast."

"Monica, my mother is having problems with Paul. He has been accused of fondling one of the girls at his high school and my mother is a nervous wreck. She feels it is all lies, but I have to confess that when I first met him he was flirting with me. One day I was taking a bath and stood to get out of the tub, and he rushed into the bathroom and looked me up and down. Now don't say a word, just listen. The second incident was when my mother was away picking up Brandon from the airport. I was home taking a hot shower under lock and key. When I was getting dressed, again Paul rushed in on me. This time he tried to rape me."

"He did what!!!"

"You heard me. He tried to rape me, but I fought hard and got away from him. I kicked him in the groin and ran. When I returned, my mother was home and so was Brandon. I tell you I never was so happy to see him in all my life."

"Did you tell Brandon?"

"No, and my mother either. I couldn't bear to hurt them. But Brandon to this day feels something in his gut because at the dinner table, he kept watching me and my mother asked Paul if he was okay. He wasn't acting his normal self. I tell you this is one hard secret I am keeping, but since Paul has been accused, I just might have to be a witness to back up this young girl's story."

"I know before you have to hurt your mother, why not hire a private investigator?"

"Monica, that is exactly what my neighbor suggested, then I thought that would be terrible. But now, here you are suggesting the same thing. Let's do it."

"That settles it! We can look in the yellow pages and go from there. I will take off tomorrow and we can do it together."

"You mean you are willing to get involved?"

"Yes, he messed with the wrong girl this time when he put his hands on you. Either we hire a private investigator or hire some men to beat the 'you know what' out of him."

"Monica, I think the private investigator will do. We don't want to go to jail with Paul, do we?"

"Linda, you are so crazy and you are right. But what if we find out Paul has a history of doing this kind of thing before. How do we, I mean, how do you tell your mother? She will be one hurt lady and like it or not she loves Paul very much."

"Monica, you are right. I've got to realize that if I have faith, it is what holds the key to opening up all my problems. I have a confession. I wrote all my problems down and placed them in my Bible. I then put my Bible under lock and key and daily I tell myself, I have faith in

God. That he holds the key to unlocking all my problems."

"Linda what a great idea, when God answers your requests, you can open the safe and mark off one by one all the blessings God did for you. You will look up and all your problems will be solved.

"Monica, I am so happy you are still here and that I can lean on your shoulder. I don't have Mrs. Carrie anymore, but I still have God and you."

"Come here girl. Give me a hug and keep on looking up. What you said, faith holds the key. I'll remember that when I am facing problems."

The drive back was a quiet one. Every now and then, I would look over at Monica and she would look at me and we both let out a big devious chuckle. I pulled up and Monica got out, but not before saying, "Tomorrow, Agent Smith, we are going undercover."

"Monica, you are so crazy! Now let's be serious. We don't want it to backfire. We want to help a young lady and myself."

"Linda, you are right. But you have to see some humor in it. I know the situation is serious, but just think how Paul tried to hurt you and he is the one who will be hurting in the end."

"Or my mother, Monica, I have to think of her, too. It is not just getting Paul back for what he tried to do to me, but it is also about trying to get him help if we find him to have a problem around young girls."

"Linda, you are right. I'm sorry. I will see you about 10 o'clock."

"Monica, I'll be here and thanks for all your help."

Monica fanned her hand at me and made her way to her front door. I slowly drove home to see what was facing me now. I pray my mother is looking and feeling a little better since I'm here to support her.

As I pulled up, I noticed Paul's car was gone. Good, I have some time to talk to my mother in peace. I rung the doorbell and waited. By the time I remembered my mother had given me a key she answered the door. She was dressed in silk pink pajamas with a matching robe. She looked beautiful from the neck down. If you looked in her face, you would think you were looking at someone who was diagnosed with a chronic disease. She looked just terrible, which made my heart bleed to see her in this condition. I leaned over and kissed her on the forehead and held her close. She needed this comfort because the tears started to flow. I found my eyes welling up, too, but I fought back the tears. I knew I had to be strong for her and I had a plan to fulfill.

We walked over to the living room sofa and I kept my arms around her. All I could do was to keep saying to her that God will work it out. She had to be strong and stay prayerful. I reminded her that God was there when she gave up drinking. He has healed her cancer and now He would give her strength for this journey with Paul.

Mother raised her head and said, "Linda, why would this girl lie about Paul? He is a decent man. He loves his students. He would never do an unthinkable thing like this. Please tell me why?"

I swallowed my pride, took a deep breath and said, "Mother, I don't know but the truth will come out and just ask God to keep you strong for whatever the outcome."

Mother looked in my eyes and said, "What did you say? Stay strong for whatever the outcome! What are you talking about? You sound like Paul is guilty!"

"No, mother, I wasn't there. But I'm only saying you need to try and get hold of yourself and wait and see what happens. You are all upset and look at him. He isn't missing any meals and he is really acting like nothing has happened"

"You wait a minute right now! You don't know how Paul is taking this. Remember, you just got here today. In fact, you don't know him at all! Linda, I'm going to bed. You're upsetting me and I am in no mood for this. I thought you were coming here to lend support, not to pass judgement. Good night!"

Before I could say I was sorry, mother was walking towards her bedroom. I found myself sitting there with a puzzling look on my face saying to myself, 'What in the world has just happened?' Now I had to put my foot in my mouth. Just maybe I should call it quits and go on back to Atlanta and let her find out that her precious Paul is a child molester.

I rushed to my old bedroom to call Monica, but I had to first get a cold glass of water. I kept replaying that scene over in my mind. What just happened? Mother is living in denial, so a private investigator is just what she will need. She needs to see Paul's guilt in black and white.

I called Monica. She was stunned when I told her how weird my mother was acting. She tried reassuring me that my mother is just hurt and lashing out at anyone who gets in her path. I found myself telling her, "Why me?" I am only here to help and prove to my mother that Paul does have a problem and she has to deal with it. I don't want to pressure her. Lord knows I don't want her drinking again. That almost killed her. While I was on the phone, I heard the front door and I asked Monica to hold the phone while I lock my bedroom door. When I returned, Monica asked if I was that paranoid. Did I really think he would come into my room while my mother was in the house? I told her I didn't put anything past him, but I plan to keep my guard up while I am here this time. I ended the conversation with, "See you tomorrow, Agent Monica."

Chapter Five

I reached in my luggage to locate my small study Bible. I knew I needed to hear from God. I fumbled through Psalms, Proverbs, and Matthew. I was about to close the Bible when somehow it stopped where I had a marker. It landed in Isaiah, Isaiah 43. *When thou passest through the waters, I will be with thee: and through the rivers, they shall not overflow thee: When thou walkest through the fire, thou shalt not be burned; neither shall the flame kindle upon thee.*

I finally shut the Bible, closed my eyes and whispered, "Thank you God. In thee do I put my trust; save me from all them that persecute me, and deliver me from this evil." I couldn't remember all of the 7th Psalm, but I felt in my heart that God knew I needed Him for my strength, and that I was placing all my trust in Him.

At that very moment, a chill ran over my body. A chill I had never felt before. It made me sit up and look around the room. Nothing was out of place and my door and windows were shut. I almost said to the wind, "Is that you Mrs. Carrie? Are you telling me not to hire this detective tomorrow? Or are you telling me that if I dig up trouble, am I strong enough to handle what he might dig up on Paul."

I reached for the phone to call Monica and decided to let her sleep. Just because I couldn't sleep it was no reason to disturb her. I put on my pajamas and got down on my knees for a word of prayer. I asked God to guide my footsteps and lead me in the right direction. I didn't want to hurt Paul or my mother. I just wanted to either prove this young lady right or wrong. As I prayed, my eyes started to well up with tears. Just to think, a few weeks ago my mother was one happy lady. And now, this accusation about Paul is deeply hurting her and to see her like this is just painful to me. I wiped my eyes and got into bed. I knew this was going to be a sleepless night.

I must have fallen asleep and had a dreadful nightmare. I jumped up and found my pajamas soaking wet and sticking to my clammy skin. I dreamed my mother had a heart attack and was taken to the hospital. I rode in the ambulance with her and watched her take her last breath. I kept beating her on the chest trying to get her to breathe. I saw Paul in the front seat looking back laughing and shouting that I belong to him now, that I had no family just him. He had a creepy laughter and kept shouting that I was going to have to stay with him and never leave. All I could hear was that creepy laughter.

I immediately removed my wet pajamas and put on a pair of shorts and a t-shirt. I didn't want to leave my room and chance waking anybody. At this point, all I could think about is should I or should I not hire this detective tomorrow. I lay down and looked at the large digital numbers on the clock that was sitting on my night stand. The time was now 2 a.m., time for me to be good and asleep. I watched the numbers down to the next minute, next minute, and finally my eyelids got heavy. I looked again and the clock read 3 a.m., I closed my eyes and fell off to sleep.

I heard footsteps and voices, not to mention that the sun was peeking through my window shades. I looked at the clock - 9 o'clock. Oh no, why didn't my mother wake me or Monica called me. I unlocked my door to find mother sitting at the table fully dressed with a hot cup of coffee directly in the front of her. Paul was sitting next to her with the same. I thought that was odd. No food on the table. In fact, I didn't smell anything cooking. I walked in and said my good mornings and headed for the bathroom to freshen up. When I came out dressed, I questioned mother about breakfast and she informed me that they both had very little appetite and decided on cold cereal and coffee. I knew mom didn't have an appetite, but Paul ate that BBQ that I brought last night like he hadn't eaten in weeks.

I left them alone and went into the kitchen for a glass of cold Florida orange juice and a quick slice of toast. While toasting the bread, I called Monica to see if our plans were still the same. Monica answered the phone with enthusiasm in her voice. I asked her how she slept last night? She said she had a dream that we hired a woman and she dug up all kind of goodies on Paul and that we were able to use our findings in court. We did so well that the prosecutor wanted to hire us to work on some of his old cases. I didn't want to tell her about my nightmare. I just told her that after breakfast, we would head downtown to see which private investigator would take my case.

I went back into the dining room. Paul was still at the table and mother was gone. I went into her room looking for her and she wasn't there. I got a little nervous being in the house with him alone. I was about to try the backyard when Paul said,

"Linda, are you looking for your mother?"

"Why yes, is she out back?"

"Yes, she is working in her rose garden."

"Thanks."

I rushed past Paul and carried my toast and orange juice out to sit on the step and try to start up a light conversation.

"Mother, your roses are just beautiful."

"Thanks, Linda."

Mother kept watering her flowers. She acted like I really wasn't there. I figured I would cut my losses and leave. I told her I was on my way to pick up Monica and that I would see her later that afternoon. She never even asked where I was going and what time I would be back. I think she was angry because of what I said yesterday about Paul acting like nothing is wrong. She is taking this molestation accusation harder than he is.

I looked at my watch and noticed it was already 10 o'clock. I rushed into my room, reached for my purse, and headed out the door. Paul was getting up from the table and he looked at me with that sly grin and winked. I just turned my head and walked out the front door. I wanted to say so bad to him God is watching you, and you will get your due justice in the end. But no, I just walked to my car.

When I arrived at Monica's, she was standing out front with one hand on her hip and shaking her finger at me.

"Look, I know I said 10 o'clock, but I had to eat something. I know we will get a bite after our meeting, so don't say a word, just get in it."

"Girl, I'm so excited I feel like a spy. I started to wear an all black pantsuit with a white shirt and tie so I could be dressed like an FBI agent."

"Monica, you are so crazy! Now, I want you to take this thing serious. You must know the impact this will have on my mother and she is already acting cold towards me. If we can dig up some dirt, my thing is how can I get her to read it? Will she really hate me?"

"Girl, your mother is stronger than you think. She might be upset at first, but the truth will open her blinded eyes and she will be so grateful to you that she found him out in such a short time of marriage. Just think, what if she had been married to him for years and found out he has a problem with young girls and she had invested all her time and energy with him."

"Monica, no matter how you say it, if my mother finds out that I hired a private investigator to snoop on her precious husband, she will put me out of her life forever. I tell you she loves this man more than life itself. I know I have to do what I feel is right. I need to do this for the young girl in that school. Her reputation is on the line, too. I would hate for her to be telling the truth and Paul gets away again."

"I'm with you to the end. No matter what the outcome. Linda, remember we are true friends. Now, here is a list of private investigators. First, let's try the one downtown on Church Street. Next, we can try the one on Ashley Street."

Chapter Six

We pulled on the side of a stone-colored brick building and parked. I looked at Monica and said, "Let's do this." She smiled and reached for her handle to get out of the car. We both walked in the front of the car and then I got nervous. I said, "Monica, wait! Let me have a word of prayer first. I just want to do what is right and well with God. Father in heaven, please direct my words. Lord, if this isn't the man for the job, please show me so I can move on to the next name on the list. Lord, I want to do what is right and I have made peace with myself that I am not doing this for me, but you, my mother and that little girl. Lord, I thank you for what you are about to do. Thank you."

Monica smiled and said, "Okay, you've prayed, so let's do this thing."

We walked up to this large wooden door and I turned the knob, but it wouldn't open. I looked at Monica and she looked at me, so I tried it again. Still the knob wouldn't budge. There was a sign in the window "Closed and will not reopen for three weeks." Monica and I just laughed so hard and long.

"What are we doing?"

"Linda, we are going to hit the next name on the list that is what we are doing."

We rushed back into the car and followed the sign around to Ashley Street. We passed the building and had to make a right turn and come back. Not a word was exchanged in the car. I pulled in the front of the building. We noticed it was a large white office building with beautiful windows. I looked at Monica and she said, "This will cost us a bundle."

I smiled and rushed to the door. We went into the lobby to look at the directory to see if the private detective was even in business. We noticed on the second floor, Lawson & Lawson. Monica and I took the elevator and headed up. We arrived and were directed by the sign to make a left to Room 202. I opened the door and there sat a beautiful, blond, petite receptionist. She was on the phone, but she cut her conversation short.

"May I help you ladies, please?"

"Yes, I'm Linda and this is my friend, Monica. We need to hire a private investigator."

"We have Fred Lawson, and his sister, Melissa Lawson. Would you like a lady or a man?"

Monica pulled me to the side and said, "Girl, this was in my dream. I told you we hired a lady and what happened."

"Monica, stop being so crazy, I will let the receptionist choose. Miss, are they both in today?"

"No, Melissa broke her arm and she still has two more weeks before returning to work. Now, if your case isn't of an urgent nature, you might want to wait for her, otherwise, Fred is in now."

"We would like to meet with Fred."

We watched as she picked up the phone and announced that we were in the outer office waiting to meet with him. Out walked a man to be about 4 feet tall. Monica almost burst out laughing, but I didn't think anything was funny at all. All I wanted to know was he good at his job and how much it was it going to cost me.

Monica and I shook his small hand and followed him into his office. He talked about himself and gave us some background history on his company. He then reached into a folder and passed me a sheet of paper. The sheet had his fees listed, which I thought weren't too extravagant. He then asked the nature of my visit and fired off a bunch of questions. He asked me so many questions about Paul, which I really couldn't answer. The only thing I knew about Paul was his middle name began with the initial L. He said that information was pertinent and he needed it to start the investigation. We finished our talk with me signing papers and I left on the note that I would find out Paul's middle name. Monica expressed that she was there only for support, so therefore she really didn't have any questions for this man. He climbed off his seat and walked us to the door. His last words were that he will be in touch and very discreet about it.

No sooner had we gotten into the car than Monica said she was pleased after talking to him. However, when she first took a look at him she almost lost her tongue. I told her never judge a book by its cover. He just might be one powerful private investigator. We decided to leave and head for lunch. We passed by McDonalds, Dairy Queen, and Steak-n-Shake when the car seemed to automatically turn into the parking lot. I yelled "taco salad for me!" Monica yelled, "A double steakburger with fries and a stiff strawberry milkshake." We rushed into the restaurant and were immediately seated. The hostess forgot to ask smoking or non-smoking, but she escorted us to the non-smoking section. A young man came to our table, took our beverage order and left. He returned in what seemed like minutes.

"Your waitress' name is India and she will be here soon."

"Thanks, we aren't in a rush, we'll just take the time to look over the menu."

"Linda, you speak for yourself. I'm starving."

"Hello, my name is India and I will be serving you ladies today. Are you ready to order or shall I come back later?"

"No, Monica is starving so I would like to order the taco salad and another glass of water with lemon."

"I'll take the double steak-burger with everything, also a small order of fries," added Monica. "After you bring my plate, I would like to have a stiff large strawberry milk shake."

"Would you like to have another glass of water also?"

"No, I still have enough to carry me over until my shake arrives, but thanks."

Monica and I went to wash our hands and when we returned, India was bringing our food to the table. Monica said, "That's what I'm talking about. Fast service, the food is hot and served on china plates." We both laughed and so did India. She wanted to know if we had everything or could she get us anything else. We both told her no thanks, we had all we needed. Monica bowed her head while I said the prayer. She looked up and said, "Girl, you are a lot like Mrs. Carrie. You do believe in the word of prayer." I told her, "You better. You don't know who's cooking your food and these days you don't know how clean it is either. I pray and consult God on everything and I know I can't make a mistake doing so." Monica said, "Amen my sister."

We chatted about the information we received from Fred and how he conducted his business. I had to give him a $500 retainer to start the process. I wanted to tell him money was no object, but I didn't want him to think I was rich, either. I must remember I have a wedding to pay for in a few months. India came back to clean our table. She insisted that we have dessert, but Monica and I were a little too full for that. I did, however, order two single cheeseburger platters to take home to mom and Paul. Monica said she didn't mind riding with me to take them something to eat. She said she has not seen my mother since she was at the hospital during my coma. She would love to just say hello.

"Monica, now don't stare at my mother. She doesn't look like she did the last time you saw her at the hospital. She looks tired and worried. I think this thing with Paul is slowly killing her on the inside. I just feel awful seeing how she is allowing this to get her so down. I really want to ask her where is her faith in God, but like I said, she seems to be a little upset with me anyway, so I feel the less I say to her the better off I am."

"Linda, if you want I can come in, say hello, and make my way back out to the car. I don't want to make your mother feel like she has to entertain company."

"No, she will probably be either in her room, or on the couch sleeping. I think she is so depressed that all she wants to do is escape from the world. Please come inside. I know it will be alright because we will not stay long. I will tell her I have to drive you home. If Paul is home, maybe we can start a conversation with him and get his middle name. Fred said as soon as I get that he will start on my case."

Chapter Seven

I paid the check and left India a handsome tip since she did an excellent job serving us. She said when we come again, ask to be seated in her section. She promised to have Monica's stiff strawberry shake just as she liked it.

We listened to music on the drive to mother's house. Monica was quiet and my mind was on how to get Paul to disclose his middle name. Finally, my tape stopped and Monica reached and put in my new Shirley Caesar tape. She started to sing with Shirley. It was alright with me, since my mind was on my troubles.

We arrived in the front of mother's house and Paul's car was there. I felt my temperature rising. I swallowed and said to myself keep a cool head and get the information. Then I will go to Monica's house, call Fred and he can get started today. We rung the bell once and waited for Paul to come to the door. He was dressed neatly and flashed a big smile at Monica and me.

We walked into the living room and I was right. Mother was on the couch sleeping. She heard our voices and woke up. Monica spoke to my mother, so she sat up and asked Monica if she wanted anything cold to drink. I showed her that I had brought some burgers for her and Paul. I told her I wasn't staying long because I had to take Monica home. Mom took the bags into the kitchen while Paul took a seat in the living room with us. I thought I should break the ice. "Paul, you remember my friend Monica?"

"Yes, she is one of the girls who came to the hospital to see you. How are you, young lady?"

"I'm well and you, sir?"

"Oh, I'm getting along okay these days, just taking life as I can."

"Paul, I see you have your initials PLR embroidered on the pocket of your shirt. What does that stand for?"

"Lawrence, Paul Lawrence Richmond, Jr. My parents had two boys and I'm the oldest. They were never blessed with any girls, but that's okay. My brother William and I got along just great. He lives in Chicago and has three boys and a daughter."

"Have they ever been down here to visit you?"

"Yes, William and his family came here the month before I married your mother. They met her and were quite proud of me marrying such a wonderful lady."

"Well, I have to take Monica home and we are thinking about hanging out a little so I will be back before it gets too late."

"Oh, you girls don't have to rush off so soon. I'm really enjoying our conversation. I was about to ask Monica what she's up to these days."

"Nothing, just working and getting myself ready for Linda's wedding."

"Yes, that's coming up soon. Well, you girls take care and I will see you later, Linda."

I went into the kitchen to see what in the world my mother was doing and why she didn't come back to join Monica and me. Mother was standing looking out the kitchen window. She had a glass of water in one hand and the other hand hung limply at her side. When I walked closer to tell her my plans, she actually jumped. I said, "Mother, I'm sorry if I scared you. I was only coming to tell you that I will see you later."

"Okay, you have fun with Monica and I will see you later."

I wanted so badly to place my arms around her and hold her, but I really didn't know her frame of mind so I just turned and headed back to where Monica was.

We walked out. I was smiling and so was Monica. We held our composure until we got into the car and I had to be the first one to say it.

"Lawrence. Monica we have got to get to your place in record time so I can call Fred. I can't believe my timing. He actually had on a shirt with his initials, which made it easy to carry on a conversation and get the vital information I needed."

"Linda, he gives me the absolute creeps! Did you see how he looked at us when we first came to the door?"

"Yes, I told you he has a problem with young girls and now I feel we are doing the right thing getting that background check on him."

"You can say that again, the sooner we get something the better. Like I said, he gives me the creeps."

We couldn't get to Monica's apartment fast enough. I ran to the phone and called Fred. He said Monica and I were private eyes ourselves. I told him the ball is in his court. He said yes, and he was going to start investigating it tomorrow. Monica and I sat there most of the evening talking about old times. We even brought up Victoria and Calvin's death, how we missed her. Victoria was a lot of fun, but she fell in love with Calvin and just wanted to be with him. If she had gotten on that bus like she was supposed to, she would still be here today.

"Linda, remember how sad it was when we all went to her house. That was one of the saddest days of my life."

"I know, and I still feel sad for her parents losing their only child. Did I tell you I saw Mrs. Carrie when I was in a coma? She used to feed the hungry, clothe people, and visit prisoners. She said that God had great things in store for me and that I couldn't stay with her. She said it wasn't my time! I said to myself I finally found her again and she wouldn't let me stay with her. That was the saddest and happiest day of my life. At first I was angry but I'm glad God allowed me to come back, and now I can marry Brandon and be his wife."

"Speaking of wife, when will you be leaving here so I can come and try on my bridesmaid gown?"

"I told Brandon I will likely stay here a week. I only purchased a one-way ticket anyway, so I really have no specific time to be home. Speaking of Brandon, I will call him tonight and fill him in."

"Hey, you better use my phone and call him now. What if you are busy talking and Mr. Paul Lawrence Richmond is standing outside of your door listening. Then we would be busted."

"You're right. Pass the phone and let me bring Brandon up to date."

I called Brandon and he answered on the second ring.

"Hello"

"Hello yourself"

"Linda, it's sure good hearing your voice. How's things going?"

"Okay, I'm thinking about hiring a private investigator."

"You what?"

"Yes, you heard me. I need to know all I can about this man."

"Linda, if you are dead set on doing this all I can say is be careful. You surely don't want to hurt your mother."

"Brandon I'm not doing this to hurt her. In fact, I'm doing this to help the young girl.

"All I can say is be careful. How's your mother anyway?"

"She's not taking this so well; seems like she is getting worse."

"Do you want me to fly down and examine her?"

"No, if she keeps on getting worse, I'll take her to the emergency room. She is in a deep state of depression, but I was able to get her to eat a little."

"That's good and I know in her heart just having you there with her is making all the difference."

"Well, you take care of yourself and I'll call later."

"Okay, and remember I love you."

"I love you, too, Brandon."

"Now, you get back to your mother's house before it gets dark and late. I don't feel comfortable with you driving at night alone."

"Brandon, I promise to be indoors before the street lights come on."

"Linda, you are making me laugh. I sound like a parent but I'm just concerned."

"I know and after all, I'm back in the town where the accident occurred, which makes you a little nervous."

"Just a little – I'll chat with you later."

"Bye."

"Linda, what if Fred did uncover some dirt on Paul, how in the world would you break it to your mother?"

"Monica, that's a good question. I guess I'd send the information to her certified."

"What if Paul intercepts it and opens the envelope?"

"Girl, I would be busted for real. I guess I haven't thought this plan totally through. I'll just wait until I get the information then decide what to do."

"You better have some kind of plan."

"Look at you, are you thinking Fred will find something worth telling my mother about."

"You never know, I'm just saying be prepared."

"Okay, when the time comes around, I'll work on a plan then. Right now I want to watch a little of your television."

Monica started flipping channels until she came to BET. I really didn't want to hear those rap songs with the half-naked girls dancing, but Monica wanted to hear the new songs. I was in her home so I just sat there while she sang along with them. I glared over at her with a strange look and before I could say anything she yelled.

"What? Linda, you better act your age and come on and get with it."

"I'm with it, but that's not my kind of music. I love jazz, rhythm and blues, but rap is out of my category all the way."

"Girl, that's all they play at the new club on the beach. Speaking of beach, would you like to go out tonight?"

"No, I'm going home to be close to my mother. I'm watching her because she isn't taking this thing so well. Maybe I'll take a rain check on that new club."

"Yeah, rain check. Girl, you probably haven't been to a club since college."

"Wrong. I took Brandon the last time we were here and he liked it. Well, until Candy and her friend, Lynn, came to our table and just took the cozy atmosphere completely from us."

"I know you don't mean Candy who graduated with us?"

"That's the one."

"What did she do?"

"Well, we found a table in the corner for two and just as we were talking, Miss Candy came yelling from across the room. I mean she was dragging a chair and made herself comfortable at our table. Brandon never said a word. Later, her loud mouth boyfriend came along and they timed it just right. The waitress came for drink orders, so Brandon, being the gentleman he is, ordered and paid for the entire table. Lynn and Candy were getting their drinks on while Brandon and I got up to dance. Anyway, we finally got out of there before they both wanted more. So, see, I'm not a square because I don't drink and don't like rap music. I'm just me. You can say a young, Mrs. Carrie O."

Monica screamed out loud. She thought that statement was the funniest thing she had ever heard. She laughed so hard I found myself getting tickled. I really needed the laughter anyway.

"A young Mrs. Carrie, Linda, you better live and let live."

"Monica, I'm happy and I do live my life. I do the things that please me and frequenting clubs just isn't my bag."

Monica didn't have another word to say about the clubs and started another conversation about her old love, Eric. Since Michael Cunningham was old news in my life, I wouldn't dare ask her about Eric. Until out of the blue she said, "Linda, Eric finished college and is doing well. He's a principal at the middle school on the westside of town. He's excellent with the children and most of all they love and respect him highly. He has implemented so many academic programs that many of the children on the eastside of town are trying to transfer into his school district. He and I are starting to get very serious. He has asked me twice to marry him and I told him I would. I was thinking about a Christmas wedding."

"Christmas wedding! Oh, Monica, that sounds just beautiful. Let me know what I can do after I get my own wedding completed in September. You know with this thing with Paul, my mother really isn't in any kind of shape to help me plan my wedding. I refuse to call Brandon's mother. She wants him to marry Olivia, anyway."

"Who?"

"Olivia! She's also a doctor and grew up with Brandon. She is the kind of stock his mother wishes for her son to be married to. She never even met me to judge me. But no, all she sees is this rich daughter-in-law. Brandon said they were always friends and that I have nothing to worry about. He loves me and we're going to be Dr. and Mrs. Brandon Alexander."

"You go girl! I heard that."

Monica got into the middle of the floor and started snapping her fingers, and jerking her head and was acting common. We both started laughing again. I'm so happy I came to her house. Monica always made me laugh.

"Hey, did I tell you about Christa and Ralph?"

"No, what about Christa and Ralph?"

"They are still an item and making serious plans to tie the knot in Las Vegas, New Year's Eve."

"Now you have stunned me. This just doesn't sound like our Christa, the old traditional kind of girl."

"Yes, traditional Christa has changed."

"Remember in high school she was the one in the crowd who said when it is time for her to get married, she would have one of the largest weddings in Jacksonville."

"Ralph calls all the shots. Christa is like a puppet on a string."

"Are you sure? The last time I saw them on the beach, he acted like he absolutely idolized her."

"Well, things have changed. She and Ralph had dinner with us and Ralph took completely over the conversation. He kept bragging about his degrees and how he is going to make a great living for Christa. Every subject we started to talk about, he has either been there or done that. Poor Christa tried to interject and he would put her down in some way. I wanted to say Christa, you got a degree, too. Don't let this Wall Street wanna-be take your womanhood."

"Wow, what a difference. Like I said, the last time I was home and ran into them on the beach he was very nice to her."

"Yes and the relationship was brand new, too."

"Yes, you're right."

By now I was starting to just answer Monica, but my mind was really on my mother. I was thinking that I've been gone long enough and should call it an evening and head back so I can catch her up. She might be feeling like she wants to talk a little.

"Monica, I think I've stayed long enough. I better be heading back to check on my mother. If Fred calls, please let me know. You know, this is the only number I could give him."

"I know you better get on home to see how your mother is getting along. And yes, if Fred calls you know I will contact you immediately. I want to know what he's found out myself."

"Monica, you are so crazy, but I love you and it has been good for me to be here with you. Especially, since we were going down Memory Lane."

"Linda, I love you too, we are best friends and I wouldn't trade you for the world. Now come here and give me a hug before you leave."

Monica walked me to the door. She was acting like she knew I was really there in body and not spirit. I think she could see the hurt on my face and that I was really worried about my mother. She hugged me again. As we parted, I looked back she was still standing in the door waving.

"See you tomorrow."

"Bye."

Chapter Eight

I finished listening to my Shirley Caesar's tape as I headed to my mother's house. In my mind, I was silently praying that my mother would at least confide in me. I need for her to get her feelings out in the open and stop walking around with this all bottled up inside. I wanted to tell her she could very well suffer a heart attack while Paul walked around like he's the man and there wasn't anyone who would take the word of a student's over his. One thing, I'm going to that high school tomorrow to see if I know any of the summer staff.

I pulled up and noticed Paul's car was gone. I found myself smiling. I know I can get my mother to talk now and she can get her true feelings out in the open. I knocked on the door and waited for what seemed like ten minutes. Mother finally dragged her lifeless body to the front door. She looked as if she had aged fifteen years since I left her this morning. My heart sank to my knees to see her in this condition. I wanted to voice my opinion, but I thought I better let her start up the conversation. I followed her into the living room. She was sitting in the dark. I cut on the hallway light so I wouldn't disturb her. With a hoarse voice she said it was okay for me to turn on the living room light, so I did and sat in the seat across from her. I said to myself 'Lord, please speak to my heart. Tell me the right words to say. Help my mother to receive what I am about to ask her as concern and not being nosy.'

I cleared my throat and said, "Mother, have you heard from the girl's parent or the school board since you called me?"

"No, but a letter came in the mail today. It was telling Paul that he has been relieved from his duties until further investigation."

"May I see the letter?"

"Yes, it is on our dresser. Hurry up and read it before Paul returns. He is so upset that this girl is making all this up about him."

"Mom, was she one of his students?"

"No, she was just at school with some of the other girls practicing cheerleading. Summer school is in session; that is why Paul was there."

Mom broke down and started to cry. She yelled out, "Why Lord! Why would someone tell such a terrible lie about Paul? He is such a wonderful husband."

I rushed into their room for the letter. I was trying to open it so fast, my hands were trembling. I was hoping and praying they would list the young girl's name so I could give the information to Fred. However, the name was blocked out to protect the child.

After reading the letter, I rushed back into the living room to comfort my mother, but she was in the bathroom. I thought about calling Monica to read her the letter, but I knew I could tell her all about it tomorrow.

Mother finally returned to the living room. She had washed her face and didn't towel dry it well because when I went to sit next to her, I touched her cheek to press her head against my chest. I could feel the moisture on her skin. She just cried like a baby, and as I held her there, I started crying with her. It was just plain sad seeing my mother so vulnerable. I hadn't seen her that weak since the doctor told her that Ann had died. I continued to hold her close. I found myself rocking her and saying a soft prayer in my heart. I wanted God to make her strong again. I knew better than to ask her to call the pastor or any members of her church because every since I've been here, mother had been hibernating from everyone.

Suddenly, mother raised her head and looked at me with those red eyes and said, "Linda, please pray for me. Please pray like you have never prayed before. I mean pray until you know that God will make this thing go away."

I was about to get down on my knees, but I had one thing to say to my mother, so I looked back at her and said, "Mother, what if this girl is not lying about Paul? Do you really know him after all? Mother, please hear me out before you say anything. You have only been married to Paul for less than a year. Like I said, do you really know this man?"

My mother got some strength from somewhere because she rose off that couch and stood over me. She pointed her finger down at me and said, "I've been married to him less than a year is correct, and he has been one of the most respected men in our church, community and his school. If you aren't here to support me then you can get your clothes and get out. I don't need negative talking around here. I need a strong praying partner. If I wanted negative talking, I would call some of the members at church. They pointed fingers when I married Paul. They were jealous, and just wanted him for themselves."

I tried to reason with her. I stood up to apologize, but she told me to not say another word to her just take my things and leave. She said she was so hurt and disappointed with me.

I ran into my room and put my clothes in my suitcase and rushed to my car without looking back. I sat there crying and trying to reason with myself as to what just happened. I felt like the love she had shown me during my illness was just because she thought I was going to die, but she really didn't love me after all. She chose Paul over me, her own flesh and blood. I dried my eyes, looked in my mirror and said to myself, 'I will never step foot back into that house so help me.' I took a deep breath and said, "Where do I go? Mrs. Carrie, you are gone and I need someone to talk to. I mean a parent. I feel like I'm alone here." I immediately went to Monica's house, but she wasn't home. I called Christa and there was also no answer.

I decided to do the next best thing and head to Dunn Avenue for a hotel. I checked in and called Monica again. This time, I left her a voice message telling her just where I was staying. I tried to tell her that my mother and I had a falling out, but I got all choked up and couldn't finish the message. I wanted to call Brandon, but I didn't want to hear him say to cut my losses and come home. I wasn't ready to give up. I lay across the bed and cried and cried until I found myself getting sleepy. I was too tired for a shower, so I kicked off my shoes, put on one of my big undershirts and got under the cool sheets. Then I remembered to pray. I got down on my knees and did what my mother said. I called on God and asked Him for an answer. I also asked Him to please help my mother to come to her senses before she drives herself crazy. I got up, hit the light and closed my eyes.

I must have fallen asleep because I thought I heard the phone ringing. I sat up, turned on the light and it was.

"Monica, girl you sound like you are out of breath. What's the matter?"

"Nothing, when I got home and listened to your message, I immediately rushed to my telephone book to look up your hotel number. Can I come over so you won't be alone?"

"Monica this is so nice of you, but I'm feeling a little better now. I think I would like to make a call to my father."

"Linda, you are about to do what? Girl you were just hurt by your mother and now you want to call him."

"Wait, before you say anything, I feel like I need to do this. See you have your mother and father, and since my mother is acting like she doesn't want me, I feel like I need to know if my father feels the same way."

"Linda, what are you doing? What if you call and he is married and has never told his family about you?"

"Monica, this is the chance I'm willing to take. I have made up my mind to make the call and if he seems like he wants to talk, then I plan to make a road trip to meet him face-to-face tomorrow."

"Linda, I'm just so scared for you, but since you are willing to do this, please call me tomorrow with your plans. If the telephone conversation doesn't go well tonight, call me, if you want to talk."

"Monica, you are such a wonderful friend and I will call you."

I hung up the phone and decided on three things: a long, hot, shower, call my Dad, and a conversation with Brandon.

I looked around in my purse for my father's telephone number and couldn't locate it. I started thinking and talking to myself. "Now, Linda, don't get nervous and bent out of shape, just think of the last place you put that number for safekeeping." I dumped my entire purse out on the bed and went through every scrap of paper. I then looked in my luggage and then it hit me. My mother gave me the information and I wrote it on a napkin and placed it for safe keeping in the secret compartment of my wallet.

I found myself feeling a little sick about almost not finding his address. I decided to calm down and make a call to Brandon first. I needed to hear his voice. I need to talk to someone who I know loves me. I can either call the operator for the number tonight, or wait until I get to Sanford and just look up the telephone number in the telephone book.

As I punched the last number of Brandon's telephone number, my mind wondered if he could hear the hurt in my voice and demand that I come home, or would he just play it off and let me handle my mother on this end. The ring hadn't fully completed when I heard Brandon's voice.

"Hello."

"Hello yourself."

"Linda, it sure is good hearing your voice. I tell you Atlanta is one lonely place without you."

"Brandon, I can sure say the same about Jacksonville. I miss you so much and can't wait to be back where I belong."

"You can say that again. Hey, how is your mother?"

"You tell me. We got into a little argument and she threw me out of her house."

"She did what? Has she lost her mind completely? Does she know that you are still under a doctor's care, that you have forsaken your own health and immediately ran to her rescue? I tell you, if I had my way you would be on the first plane headed back to Georgia. Do you want me to come there and get you?"

"No, Brandon, I'm sorry, but I just miss you so much and I feel all alone here. I wish Mrs. Carrie were alive. She would know how to handle this situation."

"Linda, you have got to learn how to handle things without her. She taught you many of scriptures and you will just have to learn to lean and depend on God. I want you to know that He didn't bring you this far to leave you. Do you want me to lead you in a word of prayer?"

"No, I've been praying and my plans are to read my Bible after my shower. You are right God didn't bring me this far to leave me. He is my strength and I know with Him I can make it. I remember Mrs. Carrie would say Psalm 46:1, 2 – *God is our refuge and strength, a very present help in trouble. Therefore will not we fear. though the earth be removed, and though the mountains be carried in the mist of the sea.* Now that is trust! See Brandon, just talking to you has made all the difference. I feel so much better. God has a way of calming His believers right down. I'm so happy I listened and learned from Mrs. Carrie. She was preparing me for this day, the day when she would no longer be with me and I would have to stand on my own. I thank her for all the scriptures she taught me. Most of all, I thank her for living them before me."

"Linda, I thank you for being the kind of lady you are and I'm more than grateful that you chose to be my wife. I want you to know that things aren't going right for you with your mother just now, but I feel in my heart that she is secretly angry with Paul. She really doesn't know this man, and the outcome of this might crush her. What I'm trying to say is - don't take her actions personally. She loves you, but she just can't seem to express it just now. I also want you to know that I love you and God loves you. On that statement I will get off this phone and let you take your nice hot shower and read your Bible. Oh, before I call it a night, my sister called. She wanted to let you know that she is so excited about you wanting her in our wedding. She also said if you need her to come back to town to help you in any way that she's available. She has a surprise for us and before you ask, yes, she will come a few days early so you two can do the health spa pampering session again."

"Please call her and tell her thanks, and I will hold her to the spa session. I know she will love Monica and Christa. Brandon, you should see me now. Just thinking about our wedding has turned my frown to a smile. You have a good day tomorrow and I will call you the same time tomorrow night, if I can."

"What do you mean, if you can?"

"Meaning I have made up my mind to visit with my father tomorrow."

"Linda, you are just setting yourself up. What is wrong with you? You just don't go busting into someone's life. He might not even know you exist. Why don't you call him first, before you make a surprise visit and get your feelings hurt?"

"Brandon, that is what I plan to do, call him first. If he sounds like he wants to meet me, then I will make the trip. We really aren't that far from each other. Monica said she would ride with me. So see, I won't be alone."

"Good, I feel a little better now knowing you won't be taking that road trip alone. Anymore surprises I should know about?"

"Yes. I did hire a private investigator and his name is Fred. Now don't say a word until I finish. I hired him and he is going to do a background check on Paul. If he discovers some crucial information, I will share it with my mother. She isn't speaking to me anyway so it can't hurt for her to find out the truth about Paul."

"Linda, I don't approve of this. Somehow, I feel you have crossed the line. Please tell me why are you doing something as drastic as this?"

"I want to either prove this young girl right or wrong. My mother is killing herself worrying about this, and the sooner we find out the truth the better. If Paul has a history of this, then he needs to seek help and I mean immediately. I knew you wouldn't approve of this, but I need to do this. I will let you know if we receive any information from Fred. Brandon, take down my number because I know this is where I will be staying, and you have a good evening and just know that I love you and will see you possibly by the end of next week."

"Great that sounds good to me. We still have wedding plans to work on. I love you, too. Now good night, my love."

Chapter Nine

I fell back across that king-size bed, looked up at the ceiling and thanked God for allowing me to meet and fall in love with such a wonderful man. I threw both legs on the floor and was about to walk into the bathroom, when the phone started to ring again. I was thinking, what now?

"Hello?"

"Linda, did I tell you that I loved you before hanging up?"

"Oh, Brandon, you are too much! Yes, you did and I love you back. Now, goodnight, I'm on my way to the shower. I love you, too. Bye."

I looked at the phone a long time wondering if he would call again. I found myself smiling as I headed off to the shower.

After my refreshing shower, I felt a little sleepy, but not as dead tired as I was before that shower. I decided to take the Bible out of the nightstand drawer and do a little reading. I started with my favorite Psalm, 121, and read it in its entirety. I found myself in Romans and skipped over to Timothy. My eyes were finally getting sleepy. Mrs. Carrie used to say, when you try and read or study God's word, you seem to get a little sleepy. She used to say that was an act of the devil. Well, I am telling him he won tonight as I am so sleepy now. I closed the Bible and placed it back in the drawer. I knelt down on my knees for a word of prayer. I prayed that God would look out for my mother. I asked God to order my steps. I knew that I was going to call my father in the morning and I didn't know if he would accept me or not, but I did know that it is all in *God's* hands. I remembered Psalm 34:4 – *I sought the Lord, and he heard me, and delivered me from all my fears.* I got up off of my knees knowing in my heart that no matter what, God was still in control and would make it alright. I pulled those cool sheets over me and rested assured that all is well in Jesus. I reached over and clicked off the light and said to myself, "All is well, all is well."

I woke up to the ringing of the telephone. I didn't know who would be on the other end, but I did know that it was early and I was in no mood for talking. It was Monica. I asked her if she ever slept. She wanted me to know that she was still willing to make the trip to Sanford, Florida, with me to meet my father for the first time. I rushed into the bathroom to get ready to meet her, but the first thing out of my mouth was we had to eat a nice breakfast before driving to Sanford. I told her I refused to be lost and hungry at the same time.

When I pulled up in the front of Monica's house, I was totally shocked. Christa was standing there, too. I couldn't get out of the car fast enough for my group hug. It sure was good seeing her. Christa said she was not in the mood for work, anyway, and that Monica had clued her in on our secret agent thing. She wanted to be a part of it. I could have killed Monica for running off at the mouth. I played if off, but kept it to myself that I was going to have a talking to Ms. Monica when we are alone. Christa jumped in the back seat. I couldn't say a word. I just told them we would go to breakfast first then make our plans.

Everyone started choosing special places to eat, so we all settled on International House of Pancakes. After our server took our order, we spread the map over the table and marked how to travel to Sanford. Carefully reading the map, we all noticed that Sanford was practically just down the street. I said in amazement, you mean, when we took our senior trip to Disney World, I was that close to my father and didn't know it. My face was now flush and I could feel my skin start to burn. I was upset and nervous at the same time. I took a pen and marked along Interstate 95 South, a little past Daytona Beach. The plan was to then pick up Interstate 4 and roll on into town.

The server came back with our order. I said the blessing and just couldn't eat. I took a few bites. With each bite, it seemed like the pancake started to swell in my mouth which caused me to feel full. I decided to drink my water and juice and call it quits. I looked up and noticed both Monica and Christa's plates were empty. They had appetites out of this world, but then they knew who their fathers were. I'm the one who was about to walk up to a man and say "Hello, sir, my name is Linda Smith and I'm your daughter."

The waitress came back to the table with our bill. She put all three meals on the same ticket. I reached for it and so did Monica.

"Look, since you two are riding down with me, I will pay for breakfast."

"Well, you should have told me sooner that you were picking up the tab," protested Christa.

"Why, Christa, what difference would that would have made?" I asked.

She responded, "A lot, then I would have ordered steak and grits."

Monica and I laughed because that is just what she would have done.

When we got back to the car, I told them I wanted to have a word of prayer. I told them this reminded me of Mrs. Carrie. She wouldn't have dared to allow me to drive without asking God for his protection.

My Shirley Caesar tape was still in the player, playing softly when Christa had to chime in from the back seat.

"Do we have to listen to Shirley all the way to Sanford? Can we have a little Luther, Marvin Gaye, Patti Labelle or somebody, but not Shirley, please, not today!"

"Sorry, Christa, I only have gospel tapes in my car."

"I knew you would say that so here, Monica, put in my Luther. That is if Mrs. Christian lady doesn't mind."

"Christa, whatever makes you happy. I'm just glad you girls are riding with me."

"You know, Linda, I got some nerves telling you what to play," Christa said. "I'm the one who invited myself on this trip."

"Christa you're just as welcome on this trip as Monica. I need your support, too."

We rode down the highway listening to Luther, Patti and Anita Baker. I must admit that secular music did sound good.

We arrived safely in downtown Sanford, Florida. I pulled into the nearest service station to ask for directions.

"Hey, we are here already?" Christa asked.

"No, Christa you must have fallen asleep; we stopped here so I could look up my father's telephone number."

"You mean you're making this trip and haven't even talked to your father?" Christa queried.

"Well, I meant to call him last night and then again this morning. But, out of fear of rejection, I just decided to take the drive and see what happens," I said.

"Linda, are you crazy, you don't just come to a town and call someone and say I'm on my way to your house. By the way, I'm your daughter," declared Christa.

"Christa, stop it, Linda knows what she is doing," Monica interjected. "We are here to support her not condemn her."

"Thanks Monica, but Christa is kinda right. I just thought this way would be better. Anyway, I'm going inside this service station to get the telephone book and see if he's listed."

I asked the clerk for a telephone book to look up my father's number. My mother had given me the address, but not the phone number. I took a deep breath as my fingers nervously fingered through the white pages. I found Alphonso Banks, 1352 Monroe Street. I wrote the number down and then asked for directions. The clerk gave me directions, along with landmarks so I wouldn't get lost.

I ran back to the car with the information and told Monica and Christa my plans were to find Main Street and call him from there. I followed the directions that the clerk had given me or so I thought. But then I looked up and found myself lost.

I located another service station and immediately pulled in for more directions. As it turned out, we were two streets away.

The girls and I made plans. We decided that when I made the call, if he wanted to see me, then I would drop them off on Main Street and come back to get them in an hour or two. Monica was all for that. She wanted to shop and sightsee. Christa said it was alright with her. She wanted me to know who my biological father was and if it took longer to get acquainted, then I should take all the time I needed. Just pick her up at the Steak-n-Shake she saw on the corner.

I pulled into the Steak-n-Shake to make the call. I slowly got out of the car and walked nervously over to the telephone booth. I dialed the number and listened to the ring. On the second ring, I hung up. I listened for my coin to return. I said, "Lord, I'm so scared and I know you said fear is from the devil, and I know you didn't bring me all the way here to let me down."

I tried calling again. This time, I allowed the ring to make two full rings and on the third one I was about to hang up when I heard.

"Hello."

"May I please speak to Mr. Banks."

"This is he."

"I, mean, Alphonso Banks."

"Yes, this is he."

"Mr. Alphonso Banks, my name is Linda Smith and my mother's name is Vivian and she used to live across the street from you. I'm your daughter."

The phone went quiet.

Tears started to well up in my eyes and I took the phone away from my ear, when I thought I heard him say, "Don't hang up." I put the phone back to my ear. I could hear him clearing his throat.

"Where are you calling from?"

"I'm here standing at the Steak-n-Shake on Main Street."

"If you stay there, I can come and get you."

"I have two friends with me. They want to shop while we visit. The service station attendant gave me directions. I think I can find your house."

"Come on I'll be looking for you, but if you get lost just call back and I will come and get you."

"See you in a little bit."

I couldn't get off the phone fast enough. I ran back to the car to tell the girls that I think he wants to actually meet me. I wiped the tears of joy from my eyes and said, "Now let's set our watches. We will meet back here at the Steak-n-Shake in exactly two hours. If he has a family and they reject me, then you two will find me sitting in the corner crying my eyes out."

Monica said, "Come on and let's have a group hug and pray that everything goes well for you. Now, go on while Christa and I do some mean shopping in this small town."

I slowly drove off and looked in my rear view mirror at Monica and Christa. They were walking down the sidewalk ready to shop. I started talking to my heavenly Father. "Father you said in Psalm 37:39 - *But the salvation of the righteous is of the Lord: he is their strength in the time of trouble.* Lord, please be my strength; as I walk up to this house protect me, speak through me, and Lord, please let him accept me as his daughter."

Before I knew it, I was pulling up in the front of a little beige-colored house with beige and brown awnings around the windows. The house had a screened-in porch. My remembrance made me look at the house across the street. That house was where my mother was born and raised. It was a brick house with a concrete porch. I stared and thought just what life might have been like with me visiting my grandparents every summer.

Two little children came out of the house dragging their bicycles. As I looked, it made me feel angry and sad. Angry because when my mother got pregnant, instead of her parents showing love, they immediately rushed her off to Jacksonville and treated her as if she was never born. Sad because I never even got to know them. I thank God for placing Mrs. Carrie and Mr. Mack in my life. They were like the grandparents I never knew. They filled the empty void in my life.

I took a deep breath and slowly got out of the car. I whispered to myself, "Lord, here I go, please make me strong." I opened the gate and closed it behind me. I took short steps toward the screened-in porch. The screen door was open so I entered and walked up to the main door. I was about to knock when the door flew open like a mighty rushing wind blew it open. There standing before me was a six-foot-tall man. He had a dark brown complexion, with almond-shaped, brown eyes. He had a thin-shaped mustache covering his thin lips and a dimple in the center of his chin. Such a handsome man; with a few strands of gray hair on each side of his temple.

He stood before me in silence. He didn't utter a word and neither did I. My mind was saying turn around and run away, but my feet felt as if they were glued to the floor. He never cracked a smile. In fact, his expression was blank. I couldn't tell if he wanted me there or not. I just stood in fear with my knees shaking and a rapid beating heart. I couldn't stop looking into his eyes. There was something about this man's eyes. Finally, it hit me like a ton of bricks! I said to myself, My God, I have his eyes. This is my father.

We both stood in silence. Again, I wanted to leave. I was fearfully thinking we are standing here looking at each other for the first time and no words have been exchanged. When all of a sudden he tried to speak, but his voice got caught up in his throat so all he did was just reach out and hold me close in his arms. We both shared tears of joy. In my spirit, I was thanking God for just this moment. I gently pulled away from his arms, even though I had longed for this moment. I wiped my eyes and looked up and saw that he too was crying.

He cleared his throat and asked me to please come in so we could talk. I walked into the home in front of him. Each step I took, I couldn't help but notice how neat and clean the living room was. The decor put me in the mind of a man's place. The room was furnished with a brown leather couch and matching chair. The end and coffee tables were made of oak wood. The coffee table didn't have any flower arrangements but magazines were on it. I did, however, notice the small piano in the corner.

"Do you play the piano?" he asked.

"No, I've never had a desire to play."

"Neither did I, but my mother insisted on me taking lessons and I did so to appease her. I never got to use what she called a talent."

"Speaking of your mother, is she here?"

"No, my mother had a stroke, so she had to be placed in a nursing home. My father is dead and I'm an only child."

As he would talk to me, he would look at me as if he was looking at a piece of gold.

"Where is your mother?"

"She lives in Jacksonville."

When I said that city, he broke down in tears again. He kept apologizing for his action. He got up and went to get a tissue.

He returned and said, "I'm so sorry to be so emotional, but your grandparents on your mother's side rushed Vivian off after they found out she was pregnant with you. I didn't know where they sent her. I figured somewhere up north to relatives. I tried to locate Vivian and you, but I had no luck in finding you."

"I know your life went on, but did you ever stop looking for me?" I said.

"You mean did I ever get married?"

"Yes, did you get married?"

"I never stopped looking and wanting you and your mother in my life. I went on and completed college. I then went back to get my master's. I've dated a few ladies, but marriage never crossed my mind. I guess because I kept thinking that one day Vivian would call the house and let me know where she was."

I actually felt sorry for him. His parents and my grandparents hurt three people. They tried to destroy the love between two young lovers. My mother never talked about him, but then just maybe that was her way of getting him out of her system. But you can clearly see that he still loves her.

"When your grandparents died, I was away at college and my parents never called me," he recalled. "I guess they knew I would have dropped everything and ran to your mother's rescue. I would have married her immediately."

He kept wiping his eyes while telling me how he loved my mother to death. He answered all of my questions. I often wondered why he never kept in touch with my mother but that is because he never knew how to do that. I was listening to every word all the while feeling like he had been deprived of part of his life. He really does love my mother and not once, but several times he said how he wanted to know where we were.

"I wanted to know if I had a daughter or a son, but I had no way of finding out," he explained. " All I knew is that I had a child out in this big world and wanted to be a part of his or her life."

"Linda, what about you are you married?"

"No not yet. I live in Atlanta and I'm a controller at AMX Electronics."

"Wow, what an accomplishment for such a young lady."

"You can say that again. I love crunching numbers."

"Me too, I'm the owner of a CPA firm here in Sanford. We are in the process of expanding."

"Expanding where?"

"Would you believe Atlanta?"

"Are you pulling my leg?"

"No, seriously, we are looking into opening an office in Atlanta. The plans have been put into its final stages. We should close on the deal in about three weeks."

"So this means you will travel to Atlanta often?"

"Yes, for business and to see my daughter."

"Oh, I forgot, I'm getting married in September."

"September?"

"Yes, I'm marrying Dr. Brandon Alexander."

When I said marriage he smiled and showed his pretty white teeth. He had such a warm and friendly smile. He had one of those smiles that if you pass him alone on the street and he flashed it toward you, you couldn't help it but to smile back at him.

"You mean I'll get to see Vivian again?" my father asked. "I mean, walk you down the aisle? That is if she isn't married or your step-father isn't walking you down the aisle?"

I almost swallowed my tongue when he made that statement. I wanted so badly to say you mean that almost rapist? No thank you.

I took a quick breath and said to myself, Lord, help me to break this news to him gently that my mother is now married to Paul Lawrence Richmond, but I pray not for long.

"Dad, I can call you dad can't I?"

"You had better. I want you to know that I'm sitting over here thanking God for allowing you to find me. I'm asking him to never let you out of my life again."

I got up ran over and hugged him so tight. The tears started to flow again; this time we both were crying our eyes out.

"You asked me about marriage. Mom is married, but she hasn't been married that long. I looked you up for two reasons. One is I wanted to know who you were and the second reason is I wanted you to walk me down the aisle."

"You mean me and not him?"

"I mean you, dad."

"I would love to walk my beautiful daughter down the aisle. Just tell me when and where and I'll be there."

"I forgot my manners, do you want something to eat or drink?"

"No, sir, just sitting here with you is all I need."

I walked over to the piano to look at the picture of his parents. They had pictures of him in high school and college.

"This picture here is my parents. My mother, like I said, is in a nursing home because I couldn't take care of her properly.

I looked and smiled, but I really wanted to throw the picture on the floor and stomp on it. I kept feeling like, what would Mrs. Carrie do?

"Would you like to visit her at the nursing home while you are here?"

"How far away is this place? Remember I have two friends waiting on me."

"Not that far. In fact, we can go where your friends are and see if they would like to meet me and ride to meet my mother too."

I wanted so bad to say I came here to meet you, not the old mean woman who separated you and my mother. But I remembered what Mrs. Carrie taught me about forgiveness. She would quote Mark 11:25, 26: *"And when ye stand praying, forgive, if ye have ought against any: that your Father also which is in heaven may forgive you your trespasses. But if ye do not forgive, neither will your Father which is in heaven forgive your trespasses."*

"Okay, knowing my friends the way I do, they would love to meet you and my grandmother."

"Excuse me while I go into the bathroom to wash my face. I'll be right out and we can go."

My father came out looking all refreshed. He even put on his cap and walked me to the front door.

"I'll follow you back to Steak-n-Shake."

"Okay, then you can go in and get your friends while I wait in the car."

"You don't want me to follow you out to the nursing home?" I said.

"No, just park the car and I'll do the driving. I don't want you tired when you get on the road heading back to Jacksonville."

Chapter Ten

When we arrived at the restaurant, Monica was looking out the window with a large smile on her face. I didn't see Christa. I got out of the car and went inside. My father parked his car and waited for me to return. As I approached the table, Christa was coming out of the ladies restroom smiling like she knew he would accept me.

"Well, how did it go? Where is this old man of yours? I thought you would have brought him into the restaurant to meet us?" said Monica.

"One question at a time; my old man is out in the car and I'm taking you two to meet him and guess what? You two are going with me to meet my grandmother for the first time."

Monica wanted to know all the details. I told her I would spill my guts and tell them everything on the drive back to Jacksonville.

While walking to the car, my father must have noticed us because he got out of the car to make his formal introduction. He shook both girls' hands and introduced himself. He thanked them for riding to Sanford with me. Monica and Christa winked at me as if they were saying my father is alright. I smiled and got into the front seat while the girls got into the back seat. My father played tour guide as we made our way to the nursing home. He showed us his office building, his church and where he plays golf. We drove up a long winding road, then through two large white gates and there sat one of the most beautiful buildings I had seen in a long time. I was thinking to myself that this building and the landscape are just beautiful for a rehabilitation center. I told my father what a lovely place and he replied that only the best for his mother. I wanted to say that he was a good man because this was the time to get back at her, since she destroyed his love life. He could have put her into some unkempt, state institution and never visited her. But I can see he is a Christian man with a good heart.

My father found the nearest parking space marked for visitors only. When he stopped the car, I found myself feeling a little jittery in the stomach. All of us got out of the car and we followed my father into the building. As we entered, it was like we were in a four-star hotel. You couldn't help but to notice the decorations. The lobby was decorated with a plaid sofa, and several green, high-back chairs. The coffee table had a beautiful silk flower arrangement and the end tables held magazines.

We stood while my father went up to the window and announced that we were there to visit Mrs. Louise Banks. The nurse came around and asked us to follow her to the visiting room. We walked down the hallway and I noticed most of the people were in their rooms. I looked in and you could see how some had decorated as if they had been there a long time. I did notice that some of the patients had roommates and some had a private room. One lady stopped us and asked if we were coming to see her. Monica smiled and so did Christa, but I found myself stopping to chat with her a little while. She almost reminded me of Mrs. Carrie because she was a petite lady with her hair parted down the middle and a braid on each side. When she smiled, she had one of those smiles like Mrs. Carrie that would light up any dark room. The nurse was patient with me because she allowed me to spend a few minutes with the lady. I then told her I had to leave, but not before telling her it was really nice meeting her and if I came again, I would look for her. We continued to the visiting room and what impressed me was that even though we were in a nursing home, it didn't have the usual elderly people smell. It smelled clean and refreshing.

We finally arrived, but Mrs. Banks wasn't there yet. My father suggested that he could go and get her, and bring her back here. The nurse said they were changing her clothes and she would be there in a few minutes.

Monica and Christa took a seat while I walked over to the window to admire the landscape. I just could not believe this was a nursing home and not a hotel. It had all the amenities of a hotel. I found myself looking for the swimming pool. I turned around when I heard the nurse announce here she is.

Monica and Christa stood up as I joined them. My father wheeled her in the front of us. She was once a beautiful lady, but you could clearly see the stroke had taken care of that. She had gray looking eyes, a large nose, and thick lips, but her face was twisted to one side. She had her left hand under the covers, as she reached out to my father with her right hand. My father went over and gave her a big hug and a kiss on the forehead. She tried to smile, but couldn't.

She looked at all three of us, and with slurred speech she reached for me and said, "You, you're my son's child. I can see you have Bubba's eyes. Those are the Banks' eyes."

I found my eyes welling up with tears. I rushed and bent down to her and looked into her face and said.

"Yes, I am grandmother."

That did it because she started to cry and all four of us did, too. She apologized not once or twice, but several times. She kept saying how sorry she was to have separated us for most of my life. She kept trying to get the words out, but due to the stroke, she couldn't. I knew she was sorry and for that I was grateful. I had rehearsed in my mind that if I ever met her I wouldn't like her, but I felt sorry for her and could see how hurt she was. I got up and hugged her and told her how I forgave her and I also found myself telling her that I loved her.

No sooner had I got the words out when the tears started to flow in her eyes again. I reached for a tissue and carefully wiped her eyes. My father was smiling and crying at the same time. You could see he had been praying for this day.

"I wish your grandfather were alive to see you. He would be just as sorry as I for separating you from us," my grandmother said. "Please don't hold it against me."

"Grandmother, I wouldn't consider holding this against you. Most important is that we have each other now. In Matthew 6:14, it reads: *For if ye forgive men their trespasses, your heavenly Father will also forgive you:* I want God to forgive me of my sins."

"Oh you are a Bible scholar?" grandmother asked.

"Yes, I've been taught everything you need is in the Bible. I've learned to lean and depend on God to see me through every situation."

"Honey, you are a wise young lady and I'm quite proud of you. Yes keep God in the mist of your life and you will make it."

"I will grandmother."
"Now, who are these two young ladies?"

"Grandmother, these are my best friends, Monica and Christa; they rode with me to meet you."

"I'm happy to meet both of you," said grandmother.

I took a seat next to her so we could talk more while Monica and Christa sat down near the window. I think they wanted to give me some personal time with my grandmother.

"Grandmother, I'm getting married in September in Atlanta."

"Oh honey, that is so wonderful. Please tell me about this young man."

"Well, his name is Dr. Brandon Alexander and he is such a very nice man."

"Does he attend church?"

"Yes, we both do together."

"You know, these days it's hard to get young men in church. Why are you getting married in Atlanta?"

"I live in Atlanta."

"I want you to know that if God lets me live to see September, I'll be there to support you."

"I would love to have you there, too."

"What kind of work do you do?"

"I am a Controller of Accounting for AMX Electronics in Atlanta."

"You are just like your father. He owns his own CPA firm. This boy of mine loves numbers, so I see you must have taken that from him."

"Yes, I think so."

I didn't want to tire her out, but she acted as if she wanted to talk for days. She would wipe her mouth and continue to try and get a decent conversation out. My father was all smiles. He just watched us and never said a word.

The visit was great and I was so thankful to God that he allowed all three of us to live to see this day! I was thinking about my mother and how she is really the one whom my grandmother should be apologizing too. She nearly destroyed her life by separating my parents, but then that is water under the bridge.

"Well, mother this has been some day. I need to drive these girls back to their car, so they can get on the road and head back to Jacksonville," my father said.

"I thought Linda said she lives in Atlanta?"

"Yes, but she is visiting her mother in Jacksonville."

"Linda, how is Vivian?"

"She's getting along well."

"When you see her, please tell her that I am so sorry for the hurt I caused her. If I could turn back time, I would have not caused her so much hurt."

"Grandmother, I'll tell her what you said."

"Thank you."

We kissed her goodbye as my father wheeled her back to the nurse's station. I found myself really feeling sorry for her. Now she has to go back to her room and think about the hurt she caused.

The ride back to the Steak-n-Shake was a quiet one. My mind was on my mother and I guess my father also had a lot of thinking to do. I found myself smiling and thinking about the old lady's apology. And about how she wants to be at my wedding. Speaking of wedding, how in the world will I get my mother to my wedding? She isn't even speaking to me. I'm going back to Jacksonville and call Brandon to tell him the good news about my visit with my father. I miss Mrs. Carrie so much; I could tell her anything. She would help me iron out this difference with my mother, but I'm happy that God has allowed my father to openly accept me. So I may have lost a mother, but now I have met and gained the love of my father.

We arrived back at the restaurant in no time. However, my mind wasn't on the ride; it was on my mother. My father broke the silence and said, "Girls, we are here and I want to thank you again for coming with my daughter to visit me and my mother. I know I will see you both in September at the wedding."

"Mr. Banks, I've enjoyed meeting you also and you have a lovely mother," Monica said.

"Thanks, Monica."

"I feel the same way," Christa intoned. "I'm happy to have met you, too, and I'll see you again in September."

"Christa, it was a pleasure meeting you, too."

"Dad, the moment we arrive back in Jacksonville, I will call you so you will know that we got back safely."

"That was going to be my next question," he asked. How long will you be in Jacksonville?"

"I really don't know but I think just a few more days. I do have wedding plans to complete."

We got out of the car and so did he. He hugged me and kissed me on the forehead. I was about to head to my car when he said, "Linda, no one will ever separate us again. I promise you, and again I'm so happy God placed you back in my life."

The tears started to well up in both of our eyes. I told him I feel the same way and I'm so grateful that this was a successful visit.

"Linda, one last thing," he said. "I would like to lead you girls to the interstate, then I'll turn off and you go straight."

"That's okay with me."

We followed him to the interstate. He pulled to the side and waved goodbye. I honked my horn and waved goodbye back.

All the way home, the talk was about me meeting my father for the first time. I was on *Cloud Nine* and thanking God all the way. I felt normal again. Here I was in the company of my two best friends, just leaving my father and grandmother, whom I had never seen before. Wow! If only Mrs. Carrie were here to see this event.

Chapter Eleven

We made it home in record time. I pulled in front of Monica's house and turned around to thank her for going.

"Hold on girl, just keep the car running."

"Monica, what are you talking about?"

"Talking about me getting some clothes and going back to the hotel to be with you."

"Oh, Monica that is a great idea."

"Well, when you carry me home I would like to come back to the hotel to be with you, too," Christa uttered. "You know, Linda, this would be like a slumber party."

"Yes, like we are still in high school," Monica pronounced.

"Hey, Monica, did you pack your bathing suit?" I asked.

"No, I didn't know we were going swimming. Wait, I'll be right back."

Monica rushed back to the car, and was ready to ride to Christa's place so she could pack for the slumber party.

"Monica, do you and Christa mind riding to the store with me? I questioned them. "I need to buy me a bathing suit."

"Linda, when I pack, I'll get an extra suit for you," Christa retorted.

"Do you have a one piece or two?" I asked.

"I have two one-piece bathing suits."

"Good, I feel more comfortable in a once-piece."

"Linda, you are as skinny as a rail. Why are you worrying about showing a little skin?" Christa bubbled.

"Okay, Christa, don't start. I know what looks good on me. So thanks for letting me borrow it. This will save me a few dollars."

"As if you're hurting financially," she shot back.

"Christa, hush your mouth. You know I have a wedding to pay for."

"Yes, but you still ain't hurting in the purse area," she responded.

"Okay, Christa, give it a rest. You know Linda does have a wedding to pay for and since she and her mother aren't on good terms, you know she has to pay for it all," Monica reasoned.

"Okay, I'm sorry," confided Christa.

"No harm done. I know you are just playing so hurry up and get packed while Monica and I sit out here with the air on."
When Christa got back into the car, she wanted to know what we were talking about.

"Food, remember, I didn't have anything to eat for most of the day," I recalled. "I was a little too nervous to eat but now I'm starving."

"Speaking of food, it does seem like it has been a long time since I had anything to eat so can we stop for some take out?" Christa asked.

"Okay, what do you girls have taste for?" I inquired.

"Chinese," Monica pronounced concisely.

"Monica, you read my mind," Christa blurted. "I was about to say the same thing."

Monica belted out directions to this place she must have been familiar with. "Linda, there is one on the right side of the street. After you pass the next two lights, make a right turn and we will be right in the front of the place."

I did as Monica instructed and she was right. We followed the route that she had suggested and ended up right in front of a Chinese restaurant. I asked them if they wanted to eat in or carry out. I told them my hotel room was a suite, and it came equipped with a small dining room, refrigerator and microwave. The small living room had a couch that let out into a bed.

"Monica and Christa, you two will have to flip a coin to see who wants to sleep in the king-size bed with me."

"Linda, a king-size bed could hold all three of us so nobody has to pull out the couch," Monica said.

"I heard that, anyway, I'm coming to be your company not to work," Christa cracked. "You know, pulling out and making up a bed is work."

"Christa, you're too much," I said. "I'll have your combination platter: the shrimp egg foo young with fried rice and Beef with Broccoli."

"Linda, since you are ordering that, I'll get the pepper steak, chicken chow mein with fried rice," Monica said.

"Okay, Monica, I'll get the Mongolian beef, sweet & sour chicken, with fried rice," said Christa, completing the order. "We all can share when we get to the hotel."

"Christa, this is why we brought you along, you think of everything," Monica jested.

"Okay, Monica, stop with the smart remarks before I refuse to share some of my Mongolian Beef," Christa responded. "Girl, no way can we all eat this food and we forgot to order some sodas."

"I have some in my hotel room," I assured Christa.

"Do you have any bottled water?" she asked.

"Yes."

"Good, because that's the only kind I drink."

"Give me a break, Christa, you have lived in Jacksonville all your life and now you are telling us you only drink bottled water?" Monica ventured.

"Yes, my parents started purchasing water about five years ago and that is all we drink in our house," Christa said in defense.

"I bet the restaurant serves tap water," Monica cautioned.

"I guess if I don't know any better, then I drink what's available," Christa conceded.

"Okay you two the food is ready, let's pay and head to the hotel so we can eat and swim," I interjected.

We arrived at the hotel and when I opened the door of my room, a rush of nice cold air hit us immediately. Christa was the first to holler to cut that thing down before we all freeze to death. I did as requested and made my way to the table for a well-deserved meal.

The restaurant man gave us some extra plates so we could share our meals. I placed a small amount on my plate for two reasons. I didn't want to be too full when it was time to go for our swim. Second, I didn't want to spend too much time eating because I wanted to call Brandon to give him the good news about my father. I dialed the number and on the fourth ring, Brandon answered. How I loved hearing his voice.

"Linda, I must say again, it is so lonely here in Atlanta without you," Brandon said in only the way he could say it.

"Brandon, I know what you mean. I wish you were here with me, but I plan on staying just a few more days."

"How did the visit go with your father?"

"Brandon, I tell you God was in the mist of our visit. My father welcomed me with open arms. We cried and laughed as he poured out his heart and soul to me. He is such a wonderful and loving man. Brandon, what was so strange is that I have his eyes. I tell you, I was nervous at first but he needed to meet me just as much as I needed to meet him. Did I tell you that I met my grandmother?"

"No not yet."

"I tell you she was so sweet to me and apologized for keeping my mother and father apart. She had a stroke and now she is in a nursing home. Brandon you should see it, that place it looks like a five-star hotel!"

"Linda, I'm so happy for you. I was praying to God that things would work out just as they did. I didn't want you to have to suffer any more disappointments."

"Thanks, Brandon, God heard and answered your prayers, because the visit went better than I expected."

"Do I hear talking in the background?"

"Yes, the voices you hear are Monica and Christa. They decided to come over and spend the night with me. We are eating and later we are going swimming."

"Those girls are so good to you. Please tell them I really appreciate them looking out for you in my absence. Just knowing that you are not alone helps me feel better."

"I'll tell them."

"Linda, I wish your mother could see the good qualities in you. She would be able to see and appreciate the love you have for people. She is blessed to have you for her daughter. I just pray one day she will wake up and see how much God has blessed her with you."

"Thanks, Brandon, if you and I keep praying, I know God will answer our prayers and open my mother's eyes."

"Brandon, on that note I better get back to my plate. I'm starving."

"You mean, you didn't eat in Sanford?"

"No, I was a little too nervous for food, but I plan to eat light and after our swim I'm going to finish the rest."

"Okay, be careful and I'll be talking to you later."

"Bye."

When I got off the phone, Monica and Christa were making small jokes about my conversation with Brandon. They said I was blushing and talking soft like a princess talking to her prince. I told them they described it just right – Brandon is my prince.

Only an hour had passed when we couldn't stand it any longer. We undressed, put on our bathing suits and headed for the swimming pool. We were all shaped nice so we weren't ashamed of our bodies, but I put a towel around me while we made our way to the pool. Miss Christa had to be the first one to really notice that I was the only one wearing a towel. I told her Mrs. Carrie would flip in her grave because she taught me better. I also would feel naked walking through the lobby of a hotel with just a one-piece bathing suit on. Christa said she really didn't see a thing wrong with it. Monica always wanted to do as I did, so she immediately put hers around her waist.

No sooner had we arrived than several young men jumped into the pool. They started splashing and I lost my desire to swim. So I found a table with four chairs and sat down to watch. Christa stuck her foot in the pool and kept saying how warm and wonderful the water was. I walked over to test the water and she pushed me in towel and all. I was so embarrassed. All I wanted to do was to kill her. I didn't want to look in the direction of the young men, but one swam over to me. He had the nerve to ask if I needed help. I told him I could swim. I just needed to get the water out of my eyes. His friend threw him a towel and I wiped my eyes. I made my way to the steps to get out.

A muscular helpful hand reached for me, but the sun was in my eyes so I couldn't see who it was. I grabbed his hand and got out of the pool. I dried my eyes and hair. I was about to say thank you, when I looked up and noticed it was Michael. Michael Cunningham, my high school senior prom date. The very one who when we went off to college played on me, who had ripped my heart completely out of my chest. Boy, he looked great! I mean he's gone from a thin man to one who you can tell frequents the gym. I took another look at his well-built arms, and large chest. I took a deep breath, and said, "Michael, what are you doing at a hotel pool?"

"I'm here visiting family," he explained. "My family reunion is at this hotel and the event started today and runs through Sunday."

"You mean your little sister, Michelle, is here?"

"Yes, wait, I will go and get her. She would love to see you."

"Hey, before you rush off, my mother told me you came by the hospital to see me while I was in a coma. Thanks for caring."

"Look Linda, we are still friends even though things didn't quite work out between us. I still care and was deeply hurt when I was told about the car accident."

I looked in his eyes and I could clearly see he was telling the truth. I told him to rush on because I wanted to see Michelle. I continued to dry off then took a seat under my reserved umbrella. Monica and Christa were on the side of the pool smiling and laughing like I still had feelings for Michael.

After a few minutes, Michael was walking toward me with Michelle and a slender good-looking lady. Michelle was screaming my name all the while rushing towards me. I yelled for her to stop running around the pool before she falls and hurts herself. When she got close to me, she burst into a light jog. I threw my arms open and Michelle ran into them.

"Linda, I'm so happy to see you again, it has been a while. Well, a month because Michael brought me to the hospital to see you and I just cried. I tell you it hurt me so bad to see you just lying there. You were so still and when we called your name you never moved. I cried so hard that day my mother said I couldn't come to see you again. Michael would call your mother at the hospital daily to see if you had come to. I tell you when I got the news I went to my room, closed the door and thanked God for bringing you back to earth to be with us."

"Michelle, I'm so happy you came to see me and I thank you for your prayers and concern."

I was so engrossed in my conversation with Michelle that I almost forgot about Michael and the lady!

"Linda, this is my wife Camella."

I shook her hand and told her it was a pleasure meeting her.

She said in a high pitch voice,"No, the pleasure is all mine. Michelle talked about you being Michael's prom date and that you two used to be an item until you both went off to college."

"Yes, but now I'm engaged to Dr. Brandon Alexander and we are getting married in September," I revealed.

"This sun is hot do you want to sit under the umbrella?" asked Camella.

"Yes, because I'm not going back into the pool just now."

Camella started calling out to Monica and Christa to come and join us under the umbrella. Michael went and pulled a couple more chairs around the small table.

Monica and Christa joined us. Since Jacksonville wasn't that big, they both knew Camella. I was thinking to myself, should I ask them when did they get so chummy with Mrs. Camella Cunningham? They are my friends. I bet Michael has been pumping information out of Christa about me. That is how he must have found out that I was in the hospital.

Monica was saying something to me. I looked in her direction, so she said it again, "Well, do you want something cold to drink or not?"

"Yes, I'll have a Sprite, please."

She took all of our orders then Christa said she would go with her to help bring them back. I wanted so much to be the one to leave because I found myself taking several looks at Michael. He was still handsome. He was growing a beard, which made him look a little older. I couldn't get over how muscular he was now. I thought I'd better look out at the highway or across the streets before Camella thinks I'm checking out her husband. I was about to start up a conversation when Michael beat me to the first word.

"My parents are on the reunion committee so they are home preparing to bring all the food to the hotel, so if you are still around I know they would love to see you again," he said.

"Yes, we are staying at the hotel for the weekend, too," I informed him.

"You are? You mean you aren't staying with your mother?" he queried.

"No, the girls and I are kinda having a slumber party. We wanted to get away from everyone and have some fun. We also needed to finalize my wedding plans before I head back to Atlanta."

"Speaking of Atlanta, is Brandon here with you?"

"No, I came to see about my mother?"

"Is she ill?"

"No, just a few personal problems."

"Oh, Camella and I recently moved to Orlando. We are just here for the family reunion. We are heading back Sunday after church."

"Great, I'm leaving some time next week myself."

Just as I completed the sentence, Monica and Christa sat our ice-cold sodas on the table. Michelle asked us to hold her drink because she wanted to get into the pool. Camella asked Michelle to hold up because she wanted to take a swim, too. She took off the cover-up and exposed the physique of a body builder. I almost lost my bottom teeth. She wasn't just a beautiful tall lady, but a beautiful fit and was blessed with trim, muscled body. I found myself looking her up and down. I didn't have anything to be jealous about, but I didn't have anything to be proud of, either. She had curves in all the right places, which made me look like a stick doll. I looked over at Michael and he was smiling from ear to ear. I had to break the silence.

"Michael, she is one gorgeous lady and I know you are proud to be her husband."

"Linda, you got that right. She isn't only beautiful, but smart too. She is the CEO of her own advertising business and co-owner of a fitness center."

"Wow! I need to sign on as a new client before my wedding."

I let out a loud laugh and so did Michael. It was good seeing that he still had his sense of humor. He never brought up the past and neither did I. Christa and Monica started talking about what they had been up to and Michael was listening to every word. Every now and then, I would see him looking in my direction. I would smile and look back at who was talking at the time. Camella and

Michelle came back to the table. I looked at my watch and said it was time for me to call it a day. Monica backed me up, but not Christa. She wanted to stay in the water for a while longer.

Monica and I said our good-byes. I told Michelle that I was getting married in September and I would love for her to come. She was so excited she forgot her real sister-in-law was looking. She hugged me and told me how much she loved me and missed seeing me. I told her I would keep in touch. I invited Camella and Michael to the wedding, too. He said he would leave his address with the front desk seeing that none of us had an ink pen.

Chapter Twelve

I walked away feeling like all eyes were on us, but I refused to look back. As soon as we were out of hearing range, Miss Monica had to open her big mouth.

"Boy, was Michael looking at you."

"Please! I'm in love with Brandon. Michael is old news and he knows it."

"That doesn't stop him from looking and wishing he was back in your life."

"Monica, please change the subject. Michael has a beautiful wife and I am marrying a handsome doctor. I think we both are very happy with our mates."

"I still say he kept glancing in your direction," Monica insisted.

"I found it hard to take my eyes away, too. Man his body sure has changed."

"Yes, I noticed that when he came to the hospital to see you. He said he had been working out at his wife's gym," Monica recalled.

"Well, it has paid off he has gone from no muscles to plenty."

We both laughed until we reached our room. When we opened the door, it was cold because we forgot to turn the air conditioner off. I immediately took one of the chairs and propped opened the door to let out some of the cold air.

"Hey, before we take showers let's warm up our leftovers," suggested Monica.

"Sounds good to me since I still have most of my food left. I didn't want to eat a lot before swimming."

Christa suddenly showed up: "Hey, why is the door open?

What's wrong, Christa? I thought you wanted to stay and swim," I responded.

"I did, but most of the people started getting out, so I wasn't going to be left there alone. Like I said, why's the door open?"

"When Monica and I got back, the room was so cold we opened it to let some of the cold air out."

"I'm glad it's open because I couldn't open the door and carry these three plates of food."

"What do you have there?" I asked.

"Michael invited me to his parent's hospitality room," explained Christa. "When I got in there, I noticed some of his family was eating and ya'll know I love food. Mrs. Cunningham asked me to fix both of you a plate and to tell you after you get dressed to come upstairs."

"That is so nice of her; she has always treated me with kindness," I said.

We immediately threw our leftovers in the trash and started on the fresh plates. BBQ ribs, fresh greens, potato salad, deviled eggs, baked beans, and homemade rolls. We couldn't say our blessing fast enough. We all started to chow down. The food was so good. I told Monica and Christa after eating we would get dressed and go up to thank Mrs. Cunningham for the delicious meal.

When we made it to the hospitality room, it was full of people. They were eating, dancing and just having a great time together. Mrs. Cunningham noticed me and rushed towards me with a wide smile on her face.

"Thank God, Linda, you look good," Michael's mother greeted me.

"Thank you, Mrs. Cunningham. God is good and I'm blessed to be here."

"Honey, come in and meet the family."

"May I have your attention please," Mrs. Cunningham announced to the room full of folks. "Mr. DJ, turn the music down for a minute. Everyone this is Linda, Monica and Christa; they all went to school with Michael."

They were all yelling welcome and hello to us. Christa made herself welcome because she left Monica and me standing in the floor with Mrs. Cunningham while she practically ran to the dessert table.

"Mrs. Cunningham, we want to thank you for the food; it was great," I managed.

"Yes, I cleaned my plate," said Monica.

"What's this I hear? Michelle came running to me talking about a wedding."

"Yes, I'm getting married in September."

"Now, I know we are getting an invitation," coaxed Mrs. Cunningham.

"Yes, I would love for you to come. Even though Michael and I didn't make it, we are still friends," I offered.

"I'm happy you feel that way because he did mess up with you, but God did bless you with a mate and him with a nice young lady. What kind of work does your fiancé do?"

"Brandon is a doctor."

"Wow! Linda, I'm very proud of you. I know he is happy to be marrying such a wonderful young lady like yourself."

"Yes, I thank God for him."

Mrs. Cunningham needed to go and help clean off some of the tables so I excused myself to a seat. Christa was sitting with Michael and his wife, and Monica was on the floor doing the electric slide. I was patiently waiting for them both, but I really wanted to leave. The song finally ended then Monica came to my table.

"Girl, these people are partying up in here," Monica declared.

"Yes and what makes it so nice is that they are doing it sober. You notice there isn't a drop of liquor or beer in the place?" I observed.

"Yes, if this was my reunion, my uncles that come from Georgia would have brought their moonshine with them," Monica joked.

"Monica, you are so crazy."

"Well, I'm telling it like it is," Monica continued. "My parents hate our reunions. They get to drinking and then they start fussing with each other. Then to keep the fight from taking place, you have to take the ones fussing to their rooms. I tell you I will never invite friends to our reunions."

"Well, if you want, I'll get Christa and we can leave."

"I'm ready when you are," said Monica.

I went over to get Christa, but she wasn't ready to leave. She said she knew where the room was and she would be there in another hour. Monica and I said our goodnights and walked toward the door.

We almost made it to the hall, when Mr. Cunningham came over to see us.

"Linda, I've been so busy, but now I have a little time. It is so good seeing you; you look very well."

"Thank you, Mr. Cunningham," I answered.

"Linda, Linda," yelled a voice from the group in the room.

"Mark is that you?" I said.

"Yes," he confirmed.

I almost forgot about Mark. He ran to me. I couldn't believe how much he had grown. I told him he was no longer Michael's little brother, but his tall brother now. He liked the attention I was giving him. I thought, since he has Downs Syndrome, that he wouldn't have remembered me but I see he did.

I hugged him and told him it was getting late and that I was beat. I had been up early, took a short trip and was dead tired. I don't know if he understood or not, but he did tell me to see him again. I knew that meant to come and see him again. I told him I was getting married and it was very likely that his parents would bring him to my wedding. He got so tickled then, so I knew he understood that he was going to see me again.

Monica and I got back to the room and discovered that we left the television on. Lifetime had a program on that immediately caught our attention. It was about a young girl who was trying to explain to her mother about a rape case she was prosecuting.

We watched Lifetime until that story ended. Christa finally came in by that time. She was ready to take her shower and head off to bed.

We were all fast asleep until I heard some talking in the hall. It seemed to disturb me and I could not go back to sleep. Monica and Christa did not hear a thing, they were still knocked out. So I went into the bathroom to be the first to get freshened up for the day. By the time I came out, both girls were up, had washed their faces and brushed their teeth.

"Linda, I made a pot of coffee if you want a cup," offered Christa. "You were in the shower so long that Monica and I are on our second cup."

"Now, you know I wasn't in there that long," I said.

"All I can say is if there is still some hot water, I sure would love to take a shower," Christa said.

We laughed as she made her way to the bathroom. When she got out, she told Monica she left her some hot water. We waited for Monica to get dressed so all of us could go out for breakfast. The hotel had a continental breakfast but Monica wanted pancakes. Christa, being the petite one, could really eat. She wanted steak, eggs, and hash browns. I asked her about toast. Did she want toast or biscuits? She thought that was so funny! When we got to Shoney's restaurant, she got the buffet like we did. She filled her plate twice. Monica and I just sat and looked at her.

"Christa, where do you put all that food?" I asked.

"She has a hollow leg, that's why she walks so slow," Monica quipped.

We all started to laugh our heads off. Monica can really come up with some funny sayings. Our waitress returned to our table with a pot of hot coffee. She found the three of us still laughing.

"You three have been laughing since you entered Shoney's. Are you family or friends?"

"We are friends and have been since high school," Monica told her.

"You can tell you really have a good time together," the waitress said. "My best friend moved to Anderson, Indiana, and I hate that because we don't visit that often."

"You will just have to make new friends here in Jacksonville," Monica said.

"Yes, but its not so easy. See I work and attend college full-time. I use my spare time studying, no time to get out and socialize."

"Now I understand, so you do a lot of long-distance talking to your friend in Indiana?" questioned Monica.

"Yes, but she does try and visit once a year. I'm making plans to visit her this Christmas. I would like to see snow and, you know, I won't be seeing that here in Florida."

"Yes, so you better go to Indiana," said Monica.

Well, it has been nice talking to you three, but I better take this coffee to the other tables before I get into trouble," she confided.

"Nice talking to you also," Monica said.

Monica did all that talking, and when the waitress walked away her smile became serious.

"Hey, she made me think about something. Why don't we visit Victoria and Calvin's grave? But first, we should go to either a florist or the grocery store to get some fresh flowers.

I thought it was a great idea since I hadn't been since the funeral. Christa rolled her eyes up to the sky, shook her head. "Do we have too?"

"I'm thinking like Monica. I think this would be great since all three of us are together."

"Okay, you two, how will we find their grave?" Christa said.

"The last time I went to visit Mrs. Carrie and Mr. Mack's grave, the old caretaker was there. So I know if he is there he will direct us."

"What if he isn't there?" Christa wanted to know.

"Come on Christa, let's go and see. We did promise to visit them at least once a year," urged Monica.

"Well, why does it have to be today?" Christa demurred.

"Come on, Christa, we all miss them! And you should be willing go," Monica cajoled.

"Okay, Monica, since it's your suggestion, you call the graveyard to see if they would give us the general direction of their graves," I said.

"You ain't said nothing but a word," Monica retorted. "I'll go to the counter to get the telephone book and make the call. You two stay here and wait until I come back with the directions."

Monica came back all smiles with a large sheet of paper. "Okay, I got the directions so we can head out to either the nearest florist or the grocery store," she said. "There is a grocery store four red lights up on the left hand side of the street."

Our waitress came back and wanted to know if everything was okay. We told her yes and that we had to leave before Christa starts eating again. She told us to come back and mentioned that it had been a pleasure serving us.

We drove to the grocery store and when we got there, we found beautiful bunches of freshly cut flowers. We purchased two bunches each and placed them in plastic containers.

"Hey, let's write our names on the cards, so their parents will know that we have visited with them," said Monica.

"Monica, that is such a stupid idea," shot back Christa. "What if it rains? Then they won't know we were there."

"Christa what is your problem?" Monica wanted to know.

"I guess, I miss Victoria so much." Christa revealed. "I often think about all the fun we use to have and it's just plain hard on me."

"Okay, you two," I intervened. "We don't need to write our names on the cards. When their parents see the new flowers, they will know someone came by to pay their respects."

"You're right, Linda. I'm sorry Monica," apologized Christa.

"Hey, no need to apologize, I understand where you are coming from," said Monica.

We arrived and no caretaker was in sight. It was a good thing Monica called to get the location. She kept telling me to drive on, make a left here, then a right. Finally, she told us to get out and walk. The graves were somewhere in this vicinity.

We got out and split up. We were reading all the headstones. Christa yelled, "Hey, I found them." We ran over and she was right, there was Victoria and Calvin's headstones.

Monica was the first to speak. "Victoria, we miss you so much; you were a lot of fun to be around. I know you are in heaven cheering for God. You know you were a great cheerleader."

She started to cry, so Christa and I were silent. Christa started to wipe her eyes. I found myself crying, too. This is so sad for us to be here visiting two of our classmates. I placed the flowers on both graves and suggested we hold hands for a word of prayer.

"Dear heavenly Father," I began. First of all, we thank you for allowing us to live to see a new day. Lord, we thank you for all the blessings you have given us. We thank you for allowing us to have such a close friendship and we thank you for our parents. Now Lord, this is sad for us because we miss our dear friends, but we know they are resting in heaven with you. Lord, we ask you to keep your loving and protecting arms around us and help us to continue to be obedient, God-fearing, young adults. Lord, thank you again for everything. These and all blessings we ask in your name. Amen."

After my prayer, we headed back to the car. I wanted to visit Mrs. Carrie and Mr. Mack's grave, but what I had to say to them was just between us. It was not for Monica and Christa's ears.

"Okay listen, we have eaten, cried and had a beautiful day. Why not take a ride down to the beach?" Monica asked Christa and me.

"Monica, you and Linda can, but as for me I need to head on home. Ralph has made plans for today," said Christa, bowing out.

"So it's like that? You don't want to be with us any longer?" Monica jested.

"Come on, Monica, I've had fun, but Ralph made plans way before now," answered Christa. Please understand, you know I love you two."

"I know, I'm just jerking you around. Go on and have fun with Ralph," Monica admitted.

We dropped Christa off at her house and headed to Monica's house. We listened to the music while traveling. My mind wasn't on the music, but on my mother. I wanted so badly to pick up the phone and call just to hear her voice. I wanted to say how sorry I was, but then I knew in my heart that she needed the space. I think she wasn't really angry with me, but afraid of what she just might find out about Paul.

Next, I pulled up in the front of Monica's house. Monica got her mail and we went inside her nice cold house. Monica went straight to her answering machine to listen to all of her messages. I tried to act as if I wasn't listening, but I was, just in case one was from Fred. I was a little disappointed when I heard the machine say "end of messages."

Monica said, "Well, that means Fred is still on the case."

"Yes, I guess it has only been a few days and who knows how long this kind of snooping takes," I said.

Monica asked about my plans. "Will you stay here until you get some information from him or go back home and correspond long distance?"

"I will probably stay for a few more days then leave. Since my mother doesn't want me around her, I will go back and work on my wedding. You know, I only have a few more weeks before returning to work. Monica, this is a learning experience for me. Either Fred will dig up some dirt on Paul or he won't. I pray, for my mother's sake, what Paul tried to do to me was an isolated incident. On the other hand, if he has done this in the past, I want to know so I may help the young girl prove her innocence."

"Linda, speaking of innocence, what if you find out he is not so innocent. How will you relay all your findings to your mother?"

"Monica, that's a good question. I think I would pray about it first. Then I would call my mother and tell her to expect a package in the mail from me. I would leave it up to God. I would then put my time and energy into working on my wedding. I love my mother, but if she insists on being blinded by the love she has for Paul, then so be it. I just pray that God will open her eyes to the truth. I really would hate for my mother to be putting her life on hold for a man who doesn't deserve her. Monica, I tell you one thing. You might be able to fool some people some of the time, but you can't fool God. Paul is a deacon in their church and God will not allow him to hold an important office like that and have lust in his heart for young girls. God will pull the sheet off of him and everyone will know what kind of person he is."

"Wow, Linda! You didn't have to go so deep with your conviction. I just wanted to know how you would break the news to your mother. You went deep and brought the Lord into it."

"Monica, I mean it. This thing goes deep with me and like I said, if he hadn't tried to rape me then I would have thought the first incident was an accident. But then he tried to rape me... I tell you I'm a child of God and he messed with the wrong one now. I want to see him where he belongs and that is not around girls. If he has a problem, then he needs help and I'm the one to see to it that he gets it."

"Linda, let's change the subject. Your entire demeanor is changing and I wanted us to have another fun day and not let Paul ruin it for us. Hey, want to take in a movie? As you see, I'm free for a while since Eric's job has sent him out of town for the next five days, so we can hang out. I know. Why don't you check out of the hotel and stay here with me. I have an extra bedroom and it won't cost you anything."

"That's a great idea. Let's head back to the hotel and I will check out and come back here. I'll call Brandon to let him know that I'm here with you."

"Do you want to go to Mrs. Carrie's old church tomorrow?" asked Monica.

"Yes, first I was thinking about attending my mother's church, but then she just might not be there. I wish I had the nerve to call her, but I know from past experiences she can be mean and say some hurtful things. I have feelings too. Let's go and get my things, come back here and watch some movies."

"I've got one better than that. Let's go and get your things and take in a movie," Monica said.

"Okay, sounds good to me!"

We were about to head out when the phone started to ring. I stopped in my tracks hoping it was for me. I then heard Monica say to Eric something about no, Linda and I were getting ready to go to see a movie. Again, I was hoping in my heart that it was Fred with some information. Monica said her goodbyes to Eric and looked in my direction. She said, "Linda, from the expression on your face, you thought it was Fred, didn't you?"

"Yes, I did. How long does it take someone to find some information on a person? Looks like he would just call me to let me know where he is on the case, instead of letting me hang on daily. I just wish he would call and say something."

"Linda, what is he to do? Call you to say that he is still on the case and for you not to worry that he isn't taking you for a ride. No, he probably wants to meet with you when he has some concrete information to give you. Now be patient and wait. Let's get you checked out and head to the movies."

Chapter Thirteen

As we got closer to the hotel, we couldn't help, but to notice all the fire trucks and the water hoses lying across the streets. When we got there, we saw that the hotel I was staying in was on fire.

"Monica, look the hotel where I am staying is on fire! Oh my God, I pray that no one is hurt. Oh gosh what about my things! I pray they didn't get burned.

"Linda, please don't get upset before you know what is really happening. Look, in fact, the firemen are coming from the other end of the hotel near the restaurant."

We got out of the car, but the firemen wouldn't allow us to get too close to the scene. I asked one of the ladies dressed in a hotel uniform what happened. She said the restaurant caught fire and part of the hotel has water and smoke damage. She said the hotel manager made an announcement that if the guests wanted to they could stay at the hotel across the street and he will pick up the tab. I told her I wanted to checkout. She pointed in the direction of the manager so I could tell him I was checking out and would rather stay with a friend.

After the firemen gave the okay, the manager was allowed to enter the building. We patiently waited for what seemed like hours. Finally, he came out and announced that the guests who wanted to stay across the street should please line up. The manager said I wasn't going to be charged for the day. He apologized for any inconvenience. He said if my clothes were full of smoke to have them cleaned, send him the bill and he would file a claim with his insurance company and send me a check for my expenses. He had one of the bellboys to escort me to my room. When we got to my room, everything was in place and you could vaguely smell the smoke.

Monica and I had experienced enough excitement for one day so we decided to skip the movie. I needed to drop off some of my clothes at the cleaners and wash the others at her house. My plans were to either go shopping or I would have to wear something of Monica's to church the next day.

After washing my clothes, I went into Monica's guest room to watch a little television. Finally, I cut the TV off and got on my knees for a word of prayer. Afterwards, I called it a night.

"Good Morning, Holy Spirit. Lord, I thank you for allowing me to wake up and see the dawn of a brand new day," I prayed when I woke up on Sunday morning.

My mind was on the goodness of the Lord and how thankful I was that the fire started in the restaurant and not in one of the guest rooms. Even though my room was a smoke free one, I couldn't help but to notice the room right across the hall was a smoking room. The guest could have fallen asleep with the cigarette in his hand. I started to smile to myself thinking of what an awesome God we serve, for not allowing that to happen.

I got down on my knees to spend a little quality time with God. My mind reflected back on some of the scriptures Mrs. Carrie had taught me. She would say if you feel lonely, read St. John 14:18: *I will not leave you comfortless; I will come to you.* Also read Genesis 28:15: *And, behold, I am with thee, and will keep thee in all places wither thou goest, and will bring thee again into this land; for I will not leave thee, until I have done that which I have spoken to thee of.*

If in Fear, she would say, read Isaiah 41:13: *For I the Lord thy God will hold thy right hand, saying unto thee, Fear not; I will help thee.* Also in II Timothy 1:7- *For God hath not given us the spirit of fear; but of power, and of love, and of a sound mind."*

I was about to get up off of my knees, when I could actually feel the presence of Mrs. Carrie kneeling down beside me. I looked over and saw the shadow of Monica in the doorway.

"Linda, that is remarkable seeing you on a bright, sunny, Sunday morning giving God some much needed praise. Girl, that's why God is good to you. When you take quality time to spend it with Him, it doesn't go unnoticed. He is looking and smiling at you this very minute."

"Monica, I don't do this for show, I do this for God. I want Him to know that I am grateful for Him coming to earth and dying for my sins. I want God to know that even though I go through trials and tribulations, I know that He is standing right there with me. I'm not ashamed of Him. Romans 10:11 says, "*For the scripture saith, Whosoever believeth on him shall not be ashamed.* In II Timothy 1:12 it says, *For the which cause I also suffer these things; nevertheless I am not ashamed: for I know whom I have believed, and am persuaded that he is able to keep that which I have committed unto him against that day."* I didn't mean to get deep, but I just want you to know that I didn't get this far without giving God some of my time and praise."

"Linda, you know I'm aware of the relationship you have with God. Now, you are the very reason I don't shack up with Eric. I look at your lifestyle and know that God would not be happy with me if I lived in sin. I also think that is why Eric is asking me to marry him. He attends church and he knows right from wrong. Now let's get ready for church, unless you want some breakfast."

"No, I'm really not hungry. I'll just have some orange juice before leaving. I'm excited about visiting church and seeing some of the old members. I will wait until after church to eat. Now let me in your closet so I can find something to wear, since you wouldn't let me go shopping for an outfit."

Monica had a nice, one-piece, short sleeved coat-dress. I tired it on and it fit as if it were made for me. It was too hot to wear hose, so I chose to wear my own white sandals. Monica came out dressed in a two-piece, red and white-checked skirt set. She looked like a living doll. She matched it with red sandals and bag. Our hair was a mess from swimming yesterday. I suggested that we should either put our hair in a ponytail or wear a straw hat. Monica had a red hat for herself. She couldn't find a white or black hat for me, so I asked her to put my hair in a French roll.

Monica commented on how nice we looked and said it was like old times. She hated the fact that I was making plans to leave her by the end of the week. She asked me if I haven't heard from Fred by then would I still leave. Again, I had to remind her of my wedding. I had less than two months to complete everything. She teased me again and said, surely I can ask Brandon's mother to help. We both got a kick out of that as we headed for the front door and off to church.

We arrived just in time for the devotion. The sound of the congregation reading the devotional scripture put me in the mind of when I used to attend with Mrs. Carrie. She would attend Sunday school and be ready to march in with the choir. I hardly ever missed devotion. She would say that it was just as important as the actual service.

The old usher escorted us in, but not before making me remember who he was. I told him he was Mr. Mitchell and I asked if he was still the Treasurer of the Usher Broad. He replied no, he was now the president. It was good to see how large the congregation had grown. I took my regular seat, fourth row from the front. I was surprised that no one asked us to move. Mrs. Carrie used to say sit anywhere. Just get near the front so you can hear and apply the message to your daily life.

After devotion, the choir marched in. I noticed they didn't have on their robes, but were wearing white blouses and black skirts. I then noticed no men were in the choir. I looked at my program and it listed a woman speaker. I leaned over and asked the young girl sitting next to me where the pastor was. She said it was Women's Day and that he was sitting on the left side of the first pew. I looked over there; just as I did he was smiling and waving at me. I flashed a big, friendly smile at him. I bet seeing me made him think of Mr. Mack and Mrs. Carrie.

Monica and I stood when they got to the part of the program for all visitors to stand. We were then asked if we wanted to express comments. Monica sat down, but I stood and introduced myself. I told them that most of them knew me. For the ones who didn't that I used to be a member before moving to Atlanta, Georgia. It was good meeting and greeting the people. Some came over and gave me hugs and kisses. That was one of things I missed about that church. It had plenty of loving people in it.

The service went as it had in the past. The church secretary read the weekly announcements, including the schedule of meetings. She asked for prayer for the sick and shut-in members. She completed her announcements by inviting everyone for cake and ice cream in the lower level after church. The congregation started singing happy birthday to the pastor. He stood smiling and waved for everyone to stop singing. He thanked the people and asked them to be sure and come for cake and ice cream, that there was plenty to go around.

The speaker spoke on God's Gift. She took her scripture from Ephesians 4:11-14. She started out explaining how she got started speaking for God. I tried to listen, but my eyes were glued on the choir. I couldn't help but to imagine seeing Mrs. Carrie sitting up there looking out at me. I found myself actually getting teary-eyed. I reached into my purse for a tissue to wipe my eyes. Monica looked at me. She immediately turned her head. She acted as if she knew what I was going through. I was missing Mrs. Carrie and Mr. Mack so much.

My mind was also on forgiving my mother. I was thinking to myself, after church, we would grab a quick bite and I would drop Monica off, and go see my mother. I had made up my mind that I was going to ask her to forgive me. I felt in my heart I didn't do anything wrong, but I was going to be the bigger of the two. I wanted God to forgive me in my wrong doings so I had better ask her to forgive me.

Mrs. Carrie use to quote Mark 11:25,26: "*And when ye stand praying, forgive, if ye have ought against any: that your Father also which is in heaven may forgive you your trespasses. But if ye do not forgive, neither will your Father which is in heaven forgive your trespasses.*"

I took another look up in the choir stand and a comforting feeling actually came over me. It was like Mrs. Carrie was telling me to go and see my mother. I leaned over and told Monica of my plans. She asked if I wanted her to come with me. I told her no, I feel like doing this forgiving act alone. Paul would be out and we could hopefully openly discuss the situation. Monica understood. She said she needed to be getting her things ready for work tomorrow.

The choir stood up to give the last selection as the speaker opened the doors of the church. I smiled to myself thinking I missed the entire sermon, but guess what, I won't be rushing back to purchase it. The last time I rushed back for the sermon on the tape I was hit by a speeding driver, which caused me to be in a coma for almost two weeks.

Monica asked if I wanted to go to the lower level for the cake and ice cream or a meal. I told her I was going to say hello to the pastor and head for the nearest restaurant. I was starving by now. She agreed with the meal, but said she was so hungry she could use the ice cream first, then the meal.

The pastor was happy to see me. He hugged me and said, "When is that wedding date?"

"September."

"That's around the corner. Are you ready?"

"Pastor, I'm working on it."

"We are expecting an invitation. You know some of the people want to come and support you. Carrie was a great member here," he said.

"Yes sir, I'll mail one to you personally and one for the church. After the secretary reads it, please have her send me the number of people who plan to attend. We are having a sit down dinner and I want to have plenty."

"I'll do just that."

"Pastor, I didn't know this was your birthday so I don't have a card, but please take this."

"Oh, Linda, you don't have to do this," he said.

He looked down at the folded up bill and smiled.

"Fifty dollars! I'm glad you did."

We both laughed. Monica joined us. The pastor was waiting to go downstairs for his cake and ice cream.

"Linda, I'll see you in September and thanks for the birthday gift."

"Pastor, you are more than welcome."

I took one last look in the choir stand and headed out the door. In my spirit, I could actually feel the presence of Mrs. Carrie O in this place.

Chapter Fourteen

Monica and I rushed to the nearest country restaurant. I ordered the smothered fried chicken, mashed potatoes, greens beans, and fried corn bread. Monica said she was so sick of chicken she felt like she was growing wings. She ordered liver and onions, mashed potatoes, fresh greens, and corn bread. Then she ordered peach cobbler, with vanilla ice cream on top. To top it off she had the nerve to tell our waitress to bring her a diet coke. She looked at me after placing her order and said that she still had two months to fit in her bridesmaid dress. Anyway, nobody looks at the bridesmaid.

I told Monica I was overwhelmed by the desire to call or visit my mother. I felt it had been too long since we last spoke. I told her I was going to be the bigger person and apologize to my mother. And if she doesn't accept it, then God will not hold it against me. Monica agreed with me. She wanted me to do whatever was right in the sight of God.

The waitress came to the table with my water and Monica's diet coke. She then asked Monica if she wanted her dessert before or after dinner. Monica said she was so hungry that before didn't sound too soon. She assured us that our food was on the way, so Monica decided to wait and have it last. She asked if I, too, wanted some cobbler? I told her no thanks. I had a wedding dress to fit into.

Monica opened her mouth as if she was about to say something and then just closed it.

"Monica, what's wrong?"

"Nothing. Okay, I was thinking about what if Fred doesn't find anything derogatory about Paul, then what? How will you help the young girl prove that she didn't lie?"

"I know what he tried to do to me. And I know Paul is lying on that young girl saying he didn't try anything. He has to answer to God. Proverbs 19:5 says: *A false witness shall not be unpunished, and he that speaketh lies shall not escape.* What I'm saying is God will bring his sin into the open for all to see."

"Yes, Linda, you're right. I'm just so scared that your mother will not be able to handle it seeing how much she loves him."

"Monica, we have to leave that to God. She will have to be strong and steadfast and let God fight her battle. I just don't want her back on the bottle. It almost destroyed her and I would hate for it to really kill her."

The waitress came back to our table. She sat a large tray full of food next to us. She then transferred the food to our table and smiled.

"Here's your food. Now, can I get you ladies anything else?"

"Yes, some hot sauce. Have you ever seen someone eat liver without hot sauce?" Monica asked her.

"No, so hot sauce coming right up," the waitress responded.

"Monica, you are so crazy, but I love you. Look around, this place is packed with church people and that waitress is working four or five tables at the same time. I would have eaten my meat without the sauce. But since you got it, give me a little for my smothered chicken."

I shook a little just to flavor my meat when a man with a loud voice from the other table asked me to send it over to him. I was surprised at him, but then when it comes to your meat, some people won't eat it without hot sauce.

Dinner was delicious. Monica finished in record time. I was still eating when her dessert was delivered. Monica offered me a spoonful. I was about to get a big scoop when I thought about the wedding dress and refused the dessert.

Just as Monica and I paid for our meal, the busboy came to rush us out of our seats. He politely said that there was a long line of people waiting to be served. I looked at Monica and she looked at me, but no words were exchanged. We rushed out so some poor hungry soul could have our seats.

The drive back to Monica's house was filled with sounds from my new gospel tape. The music and the words to the songs touched my very soul. Monica had the nerve to try and sing along with the Yolanda Adams.

Finally, we arrived. I was anxious to get Monica out of the car and head to my mother's house for a little talk. Monica tried to talk me into calling first, but I told her no, I wanted to surprise her.

I popped my tape back in to finish listening to some of my favorite songs. I didn't have Monica in there trying to sing with Yolanda, so I could clearly hear and enjoy the tape.

As I turned the corner, I softly said a prayer that Paul would not be home. I wanted to be alone with my mother so I could apologize and she would readily accept it. I was looking ahead as far as I could, when I noticed

Paul's car wasn't home. I could have jumped for joy. Instead I yelled Hallelujah! Thank you, God, for small favors. I prayed for God to put my mother in the right frame of mind. I rushed to park so I could hurry up and make my visit a short one.

I got out of the car, and headed straight for the door. I was wishing that as I knocked the door would fly open, and she would accept me just as I am. I knocked and patiently waited. No answer. I banged on the door again, this time yelling "Mom, this is me, Linda."

I stood for what seemed like hours, but in reality, it was only a few minutes. But she never came to the door. I looked toward the living room window just to see if the curtains were moving but they stood as stiff as ever. I took a deep breath and made up in my mind she was in there or just wasn't in the mood to see me. I cut my losses and headed back to my car. My emotions ran high as I was feeling like I had lost her forever.

I felt alone. Carrie and Mr. Mack were in heaven and I didn't want to call my father, so I decided to just head back to Monica's house and call Brandon. I needed to hear his voice, I needed to feel wanted and not like I was an orphan. I made a u-turn and headed back in the direction of Mrs. Love's house, when I noticed her walking to her fence. I waved at her and she beckoned for me to come over to her. I pulled up, parked and ran into her waiting arms.

"Mrs. Love, I want to thank you for visiting me while I was in the hospital and the prayers you prayed for me."

"Honey, God still has work for you to do, he wasn't about to carry you on home. I tell you, he wants you to complete the job Carrie started. Come on inside, it is too hot to be standing out here. I have plenty to tell you."

I followed her into her nice, clean air-conditioned house. I took a seat in the living room while she went into the kitchen. She said not once, but twice for me to make myself comfortable. I sat on the large love seat, and looked at all of her pictures on her end table.

She returned with a slice of some kind of cake and strawberry ice cream on the side. I was about to say how did you know strawberry is my favorite, but I thought first. If she is supposed to be a prophetess inspired by God, she just might know some of my likes.

"Linda, you look good and I want you to listen as I speak. God is too wise to make a mistake. Sometimes things happen for a reason. We might not understand why, but nothing can happen without God giving the devil permission. Your mother is a little upset right now, but by and by, things will work out between you two. I am not going into your business. I just want to give you what God has given me. If you are feeling lonely read Genesis 28:15. It says, *And, behold, I am with thee, and will keep thee in all places whither thou goest, and will bring thee again into this land; for I will not leave thee, until I have done that which I have spoken to thee of.*

"I also want you to know that God will give you peace," encouraged Mrs. Love. "Read John 14:27: *Peace I leave with you, my peace I give unto you: not as the world giveth, give I unto you. Let not your heart be troubled, neither let it be afraid.* And last, not least, when you pray at the end of your prayer remember to read Matthew 7:7,8: *Ask, and it shall be given you; seek and ye shall find; knock and it shall be opened unto you: For every one that asketh receiveth; and he that seeketh findeth; and to him that knocketh it shall be opened."*

I ate and listened to all she had to say. I found myself feeling the presence of God, as she read the scriptures. I could actually feel the calmness of the words penetrating my very soul. I wiped the tears from my eyes and in a soft whisper asked for the restroom.

When I came out, she had cleaned up my dishes and was sitting just where I left her.

"Mrs. Love, I will never forget this time I've spent with you, and I know God gave you those scriptures just for me. I was feeling lonely and I'm seeking peace in my life and most of all, praying without ceasing. This is how I make it, on prayer. When I look back and see how far God has brought me, all I can do is thank him for what he has done for me. I believe my mother and I will make up and I feel in my heart that everything will work out for the best. I now feel like I can make it. In fact, since we had this little talk I am going to the dress shop in St. Augustine tomorrow to look at wedding dresses, bridesmaid dresses and a dress for my mother."

I went over and gave her a big hug and a kiss on the cheek. I was feeling like a brand new person. God had directed me to her house and I'm so glad I followed his direction.

Mrs. Love told me not to be a stranger and, God willing, she would be at my wedding. She also told me that she would keep me in her prayers. I was about to walk out of the house, when she said something to me that floored me.

She said, "Remember all that I've told you today and also remember 'faith holds the key.' "

I turned around and asked her what did she say?

She said, "You heard me," and she just smiled and walked back into her house. At that very moment, I knew that she was a prophet inspired by God."

Chapter Fifteen

I arrived at Monica's only to find her not at home. Thank God she gave me a spare key. I rushed inside and the first thing that was on my mind was to get out of her church clothes and put on my white leather slippers. I was thinking to myself that the shoes shouldn't still smell of smoke since I washed them before I went to church. I smiled at the same time as I found myself holding one of them up to my nose to see if I got all the smoke smell out of them.

I put on my nice silk robe and headed for the living room to call Brandon. I missed him something terrible. I dialed his number and the phone rang twice, three times, and before the fourth ring completed, I heard the sound of a sleepy Brandon.

"Hello"

"Brandon, this is Linda. How are you?"

"Linda, hey baby, how's things going with you. I was thinking seriously about calling Delta to come down and bring you back home. Girl, I miss you so much. I tell you seems like you have been gone forever."

"Stop it, Brandon. You know it hasn't been but a few days. But I tell you, a lot has happened since then. I'm still staying with Monica and tomorrow I have plans to go shopping for my wedding gown."

"You mean, you are still marrying me?"

"Brandon, you are so crazy. You know the wedding is still on, and I mean that more than ever." I found myself smiling from ear-to-ear, while I was trying to express my feelings to him.

"So, when are you coming home?"

"I think I will make my reservations for next Monday."

"Next Monday! Linda, I see right now I am going to call Delta and come and get you. I don't want you to stay that long. Why do you need to stay another whole week?"

"I haven't heard from Fred yet?"

"Who?"

"You know, the private investigator. I told you all about Fred."

"Oh, so you guys are on first name basis."

"Brandon, he is not my type. And yes, we are on a first name basis. If you laid eyes on Fred, you would see you have nothing to worry about."

"I'm not worried. I just miss you, and Fred gets to see you as much as he can."

Brandon let out a loud, cheerful laugh. I knew he was joking and a little jealous at the same time. I promised him to try and wrap up things by the end of the week. I also told him to look for me either Friday or Saturday. I was a little tired of sitting around Jacksonville. I could be out shopping for a place to host our wedding reception.

"Brandon, I'll make the reservation and call you with my flight time Thursday."

"Does this mean you are coming home Friday?"

"Yes, so good night, my love."

"Good night, and, Linda, I love you, too."

I just fell back on the sofa with stars in my eyes. Just thinking about the last sentences he said: Good night, and, Linda, I love you, too.

I thank God for giving me Brandon and I know in my heart that he's a good man and he will make a wonderful husband. I reached for the remote control to see what was on TV. I flipped through the channels until I finally came to a romantic story. I thought this would be just what I needed to see. Right; a happy couple. Not! That would remind me of Brandon. I changed that station quickly.

Cartoons were on and I always loved cartoons. When the first commercial came on, I rushed to the kitchen for a glass of water. I looked in Monica's refrigerator and almost lost my teeth. This child had a gallon of water, half a gallon of skim milk, half a gallon of orange juice, and some diet cokes. I looked in her vegetable bin. It had two small apples and a lemon. I laughed when I thought about how much Monica could eat. Yet, she doesn't even have enough food in her refrigerator to feed a four year old.

I looked in her cabinet and was surprised. While there was nothing in the fridge, she had every choice of popcorn - light with butter, caramel, and plain. I took the light with butter. I found some lemonade mix, and while my popcorn was in the microwave popping, I made a large glass of ice cold lemonade.

Monica's phone started ringing, but I didn't want to answer it. I said to myself let her answering machine pick up.

"Linda, are you there? This is Monica, pick up the phone."

"Monica, hey girl, where are you?"

"I'm at work; we had some computer problems and I was called in. I hate to leave you alone, but looks like it is going to be an all-nighter. Just lock up and check the back door and I'll see you sometime in the morning."

"Hey, I'll do just that. You take your time and solve the problem. I'll be all right. I have Jesus on my side and I know he won't let any harm come to me. Talk with you tomorrow."

"Linda, if we finish a little early I will call you. Otherwise I will see you in the morning."

"Bye, and take your time."

I rushed to get my popcorn out the microwave, then to check the windows and doors. I wasn't afraid at all, but I sure did wish she was there with me. I got my lemonade and headed back to the living room to make a nice comfortable place on the couch. This is where I will be spending the night, in front of this big screen TV.

The cartoons were boring to me so I flipped them off. I turned to the Sunday night movie and it was a movie by Stephen King. His movies have always been a little too scary for me, so I change channel again. I was about to flip again when a news flash caught my attention.

"We interrupt this program to tell our viewing audience that a prisoner has just escaped from Jacksonville City Jail. He is considered armed and dangerous." They flashed a picture of the prisoner and I started to ball up in a knot. I was wishing I was not alone when all of the sudden I heard a loud knock on the front door. I wanted to scream, but I didn't want whoever it was to know I was the only one home. I didn't know what to do. I could actually feel my bones shaking in my skin. I didn't know if I should turn the living room light out or what. All I could do was sit, and hope whoever it was would go away.

The knock was getting louder and louder then I heard a familiar voice. "Linda, open this door this is Christa. Monica called me and asked me to come over and spend the night with you."

I ran to the door and looked out and yes, she was standing there with her arms full. I unlocked the doors and let her in. She had groceries and her luggage.

"Girl, what took you so long to open the door?"

"I didn't know who you were. Haven't you heard about a prisoner that has escaped from jail?"

"Oh girl, that happens often," Christa said. "He's probably long gone by now. He would be a fool to escape and stay around here to get caught. I guarantee you that man is in Miami by now or about to make his way to Texas."

"Christa, how can you kid about something so serious? You better learn to take things more seriously. What if he is still here hiding out? What if he is in our neighborhood now?"

"Then Linda, I suggest you call the cops. If you are so sure he is lurking around the corner waiting to break in here."

"Forget it, Christa. I'm sorry I said anything to you about the escaped prisoner."

"Now Linda, I came over to be with you and not to argue, so lets forget about him and watch some of these movies I brought. You pick the movie. Most of them I have seen several times, but I love them so much I'll watch them over and over again."

"Christa, do you want me to fix you a bag of popcorn?"

"That would be okay, seeing that's all Monica buys."

"How did you know?"

"Because, most of the time when Ralph is out of town I head straight over here. We go out for dinner first, but we always leave enough room for our popcorn and movies."

"How often does this happen?"

"Oh, about once every two weeks; we always say we wish you were here with us."

"I know Monica wishes she were here with us now but she's trying to get the computer working so she can come home soon. All we can do is pray she solves the problem quickly, so we can be together eating popcorn and watching movies."

I was listening to Christa, but thinking to myself. With a prisoner on the loose, staying in a large house all alone is no joke. I probably would have been doing a lot of pacing the floor, looking out the windows and definitely praying. Then I would have gotten out my Bible and did a little reading. I probably wouldn't remember a thing I read because of being so scared. Then I would have started quoting scripture after scripture on fear.

"Linda, did you say something?"

"No, just thinking out loud."

Chapter Sixteen

I looked over and the television was off. Christa was curled up on the love seat and Monica on the floor. The last thing I remembered was Christa talking while we were supposed to be watching television. Monica must have come in and turned it off. I remember getting a blanket and a pillow, but not one for Christa. Monica must have come in and placed one over Christa. All I know is I thank God for sending her over to spend the night with me.

"Good morning sleepy head, why didn't you sleep in your bed? You know you have to go to work this morning," I said to Monica.

"So does Christa," Monica replied. "Christa, wake up, so you can hit the shower and make it to work."

"What time is it?" Christa yawned.

"It's 5:00 o'clock," Monica said.

"Five o'clock! I better get to the shower. I'm supposed to train a new hire at eight o'clock and I need to make it to the coffee shop first, for an eye opener. I need the caffeine and I mean I need it bad. I should have slept in the guestroom, but Linda and I were watching movies and talking and I guess we fell asleep."

"Linda, do you have any plans for the day?" asked Monica.

"Yes, I'm going to call my father in about an hour then I'm going to a little shopping in Saint Augustine. Mrs. Carrie took me there to purchase my prom dress. I want to see if the shop has any wedding dresses."

"Christa, you have a good day at work," Monica said. "Linda, enjoy your day. Me, I'm headed back to bed and I'll go in later today."

I almost fell out laughing when Monica came from under the cover. She was wearing cartoon cotton pajamas. She saw me looking at them, so she was the first to say something.

"Look I'm not married and I can wear whatever I want to bed. Besides, when I got in late last night the air was real cold and so was I."

Christa didn't say a word. She just folded her blanket and made her way towards the guestroom. I didn't want to get Monica's nerves on edge knowing that she really hadn't had her full eight hours worth of sleep, so I rushed into her bathroom for a nice hot shower.

When I came out of Monica's private bathroom, she was curled up in a ball fast asleep with the covers pulled over her head. I quietly tip toed out so I wouldn't disturb her rest.

I went in the guest room and Christa was gone. I walked into the living room and there she was writing me a note.

"Linda, I was just leaving you a note. I'm on my way to the coffee shop, then to work. If you want, we can all meet here and go out for dinner."

"I think tonight would be good for me," I said. "Remember, I said I wanted to call my father then make a short trip to Saint Augustine today, and look at some wedding and bridesmaid dresses."

"Oh, I forgot. After work I will go straight home to get my mail, change clothes and meet you two here. Does about six o'clock sound okay?" asked Christa.

"Yes, six o'clock sounds perfect. Christa, have a good day."

I went into the guestroom to get my purse so I could make that call to my father.

"Dad, good morning this is Linda. How are you?"

"Linda, it's so good hearing your voice so early in the morning. Is there anything wrong?"

"Oh no, I just wanted to say hi and to let you know that I'm still in Jacksonville. I will be shopping in Saint Augustine around ten o'clock this morning. If I find something, then I will buy it and have it shipped to Atlanta."

"Linda, that's a great idea. Hey, why don't I meet you there, we can shop together."

"I would love for you to meet me there, but I don't even know the name of the shop. All I know is it is off Randolph Street. I know there is a McDonald's on Randolph. Meet me there at ten o'clock and you can follow me to the shop."

"I'll see you at ten. Bye baby."

"Bye Dad."

I couldn't hang the phone up quickly enough so I could praise God. Oh God, I thank you again for letting me find my father and for him accepting me the way he has. I was feeling a little hungry and knew there wasn't anything in the house to eat, except popcorn and more popcorn.

I quietly pulled the door shut and made my way to the car. I wanted a nice hot breakfast. I thought about going to Mrs. Williams' for breakfast then I quickly said to myself no. I drove across town and pulled into Shoney's Restaurant. I knew they had a hot buffet and lots of good coffee.

After a nice hot breakfast, I started my drive to St. Augustine. The trip reminded me of Mrs. Carrie. The last time I made the drive she was sitting next to me. She enjoyed watching the highway, listening to my gospel tapes, and every now and then she would strike up a conversation. I honestly found myself looking over to the passenger side of my car. Thinking of her smile and laughter instantly put me in a sad mood. My eyes started to fill with tears. I had to swallow hard to fight back the tears. I took a deep breath; pushed in my gospel tape and tried to sing alone with Yolanda Adams.

Finally, a reached a sign: Welcome to St. Augustine, the oldest city in Florida. Thank you God I made it, now to find Randolph Street. I drove a few blocks and started talking to myself. "Randolph should be the next street over if my memory serves me well." I made a right turn and yes it was. I saw the golden arches as I drove down Randolph. I pulled in and parked. As I entered McDonald's, there in the corner sat my Dad. I called out to him, "Dad I'm here." He ran over and hugged me and kissed me on the cheek.

"Linda, you made it. How was the drive?"

"It wasn't bad at all. I guess most of the drivers are at work."

"I'm just having a cup of coffee, do you want to join me."

"No thank you, I've had plenty. Remember the two girls you met? Well I'm staying with Monica and she was called into work yesterday. She reminded me to make sure the doors and windows were locked because she might have to work all night. Just as it started to get dark, a news flash announced a prisoner had escaped from Jacksonville Jail. Immediately, my vivid imagination started working overtime. Suddenly, I heard a knock on the front door and I was too scared to open it. The knock got louder and then I heard Christa calling me. I was never so glad to see her. We stayed up most of the night eating popcorn and watching movies. So you see, I'm a little tired today. Monica doesn't have any food so I went out this morning for breakfast. I had the buffet at Shoney's and a pot of coffee."

"Linda, a pot?"

"Yes, a pot." We both shared a laugh about me drinking so much coffee.

My Dad finished his coffee and said he would follow me to the little shop.

When we arrived, he got out of his car and came to where I was standing. He had such a curious expression on his face. I told him I know it is an old wooden store, but just follow me inside and see the beauty.

"May I help you?"

"Yes, is Brenda here?" I asked.

"No, she is off today. I'm her daughter, do you know my mother?" said the woman who greeted us.

"Well, kinda. She is the one who sold me my prom dress a few years ago and now I'm getting married and wanted her to help find my wedding dress."

"My mother does have good taste. Not to be presumptuous, but like mother like daughter."

I asked, "What is your name?"

"My name is Nikita Wright."

"My name is Linda Smith and this is my father, Mr. Alphonso Banks."

"Pleased to meet you both," she said.

"My wedding is in September, so I would like to find a wedding dress and also look at the mother of the bride, and the bridesmaid dresses."

"Wow! Before I can help you with such a tall order, I have some questions. What are your colors, and how many girls will be in your wedding?"

"I have one maid-of-honor and two bridesmaids. My color is lavender, and I would like to find my mother a champagne-color, tea-length, chiffon dress."

"Do you want to look at what I have on my mannequins or do you want to look in the book?" asked Nikita.

"I think both. First, let me walk around the shop and see what you have. If I don't find anything, then I will go to the book."

"Good enough. I would like to get an idea of what kind of gown you are looking for," she said.

Maybe while I am looking for my bridesmaid dresses, I will find something I like. If not, then I will look in the books.

My father said to Nikita that this was going to take some time, and asked where he could sit while I looked. She pointed in the far corner, where there were three soft cushioned chairs. There was also a large wooden table, with magazines, and books to keep him comfortable while he waited. My father smiled as he made his way to the sitting area.

I walked around admiring such elegant gowns. I was so impressed with the different colors, textures and styles. The owner still maintained her motto "one-of-a-kind dresses" in the shop. Except for bridesmaid dresses, which could be ordered out of the book.

I finally found the dress for my bridesmaids. Monica, being my maid-of-honor, needed either a different style or color. I found the most beautiful lavender dress, so I knew I needed to stay with that shade. I immediately made up my mind to find Monica a different style.

Christa and Brandon's sister, Lynda, would wear the dress with the thin spaghetti straps, while Monica could wear the same dress without the straps. Both dresses are adorned with hand beaded pearls.

I ran over to show my father so he could see the dresses I picked out for my bridesmaids. He was so happy that he could play such a valuable part in my wedding. He approved of the beautiful material for the dresses. I was about to comment when Nikita came rushing to where we were standing.

"Linda I have chosen such an elegant dress for your mother. Please follow me to the middle of the store."

My father was about to head back to his seat when I politely grabbed him by the arm and told him to follow me. He looked at me with his approval smile and followed me.

Nikita was blushing like she knew I would just fall in love with the dress. I looked and there wasn't anything in the middle of the floor. She laughed as she walked toward us. She grabbed my free hand and turned me around to face one of the most beautiful, champagne, chiffon, after-five floor length dresses. My mouth flew open because I could visualize my mother walking down the aisle in the dress. I put my hand up to my mouth. I wasn't sure whether I was about to scream or cry.

"Dad, this is mom! I tell you this is made just for her. She will look beautiful in this dress."

"Linda, what is her shoe size?"

"Mom wears a 7 shoe," I said.

"Linda, don't move; I have a pair of shoes and an evening bag that will be the perfect accessories for this dress."

I looked at my dad and asked, "Could this be my lucky day or what?"

He said, "No, not luck, but God is giving you his blessings. Linda, I wasn't around when you growing up, but from the short time I've been with you, I know you are a God-fearing young lady and God is going to reward you."

I threw my arms around his neck and said, "Dad, I thank you for that statement. You are right. I've tried to do my best. Life hasn't always been kind to me, but if I never had a problem, I wouldn't know what God could do."

Nikita returned with a box and a purse in plastic. She was smiling like she had found my mother's size.

"Linda, these shoes are a 7 and this is the purse that matches them."

I reached for the shoes and fell in love with them immediately. The shoe was a shinny, champagne material, with small pearls on the top, and the same pearls accented down the back of the heel of the shoe. The heels were about 2¼ inches high. The purse was made with the same material with a single large pearl closure.

I was so caught up with the style of the dress and the matching shoes and purse I almost forgot to ask for the size. Nikita beat me to the question. She asked me my mother's dress size because the dress was a size 12.

I almost lost my tongue. I yelled out loud "That is exactly the size my mother wears."

Nikita asked if I wanted her to place the dress in a garment bag, so I could take it with me, or did I want it shipped like the bridesmaid dresses. I told her I wanted to take it back to Jacksonville and show it to my mother.

She carefully placed the dress in a garment bag. Then she used several layers of tissue paper to cover the purse. She placed the shoes and purse in the same bag and walked them over to the cash register.

Chapter Seventeen

Nikita rushed to the back of the store to locate the sheet of paper I had given her with the bridesmaid sizes on it. I stood there patiently waiting because that was the only sheet of paper I had. I forgot to make copies. Nikita ran back to the front with the paper in hand. She was yelling that she located it. She said now it is your time to look around for a dress. I had to remind her that I had found three dresses to my liking and I was just waiting for her to place them in the dressing room for me.

The first gown was a ball gown with a fitted waist and strapless. The train was what she called a chapel length. I didn't care for the strapless, off the shoulder look. My father asked if he could come back to see me model the dresses. I told him, please do. He gave his approval, but said he would hold his final approval until he had seen all three.

I tried on another gown that was fitted, but it made me look too thin. I tried on the final gown. It was a slender fit, yet elegant and had a graceful skirt. Silky satin material embellished with beads and sequin over lace appliques. The train was extended from upper back to the floor. I put on the headpiece that Nikita had chosen and it was adorned with beads on the crown.

I walked out and my father started clapping, "Beautiful, beautiful, Linda you are just beautiful. Now this is the gown for you."

I smiled, as the tears started to fill my eyes. He dropped his head and I saw him wipe his eyes too. It was such a touching moment. Here I was in a little wooden store with my father, the man who will walk me down the aisle. I looked up and said, "Thank you God for this day."

Nikita said, "Now that gown fits you perfectly and I only have one question. Where can I ship this dress to?"

We all laughed.

I went to get out of the dress while Nikita looked for the style number to order the dress for me.

I came out of the dressing room to find my father at the counter with his checkbook out and paying for the entire order.

"Dad, what are you doing?"

"Linda, I am doing what a father is supposed to do, pay for his daughter's wedding."

"But I didn't bring you here for this. I wanted you to come alone for support, not to pay for the dresses."

"Linda, you are my daughter and I know I can't make up for all the time I wasn't in your life, but I am surely going to do my best to make Atlanta see one of the most beautiful weddings they have seen in a long while."

I ran into his waiting arms. It was a good feeling to know that even though Mr. Mack and Mrs. Carrie were dead, and my mother was acting terrible, God had placed my father in my life just at the time I needed him. I whispered to myself "What a mighty God we serve."

We left the store with mom's dress, shoes and handbag. Nikita would mail the bridesmaid dresses to each of the girls. All they had to do was to wait to receive them and the scrap of material and take that piece of material to get their shoes dyed. I told them to send me the bill and I would reimburse them. Knowing Lynda, she will probably not send her bill. She is financially able to pay, but I still made the offer.

Dad made the suggestion that a nice juicy steak would really hit the spot. Since I was hungry, I agreed with him. Dad had got the name of a good steak restaurant that was not too far from the shop. Dad parked his car and I pulled in next to him. He opened the door and we walked in arm-in-arm. Dad noticed the sign, seat yourself so we took a seat in the front. I couldn't help but to notice the wooden floors covered with what I thought was sawdust. We sat down and there was a small tub of peanuts on each table. So that's what was all over the floors, peanuts, and not sawdust!

A young petite, blond waitress came to the table dressed in a short tennis skirt outfit. She was beautiful with large blue eyes, and a nice warm and friendly smile.

"Hello, my name is Emily. I will be your waitress for today. She quickly ran down today's special, but noted our most popular item is the sirloin steak."

"Emily, what do you suggest?" I asked.

"Well, I think you should try the petite sirloin steak with the butterfly shrimp combo. Sir, I think you should try the porterhouse it's larger," she added to dad.

"What else comes with the entrée?" I queried Emily.

"Baked potato, salad or vegetables," she promptly answered.

"Dad what do you want?"

"I'll try the porterhouse steak prepared medium. I'll also have the baked potato with lots of butter."

"Sir, do you want a house salad?" the waitress asked.

"Yes, I'll take blue cheese dressing."

I was next. "Okay, I'll take the butterfly shrimp with the petite sirloin steak, but please make mine well done. I will pass on the potato, but I'll take lots of French dressing on my salad."

"I'll put your order in and be right back," she assured us.

"Here are two glasses of nice cold water. Now what else can I get you to drink?"

"Do you have ice tea?" dad asked.

"Yes, sir," she snapped.

"Then, I'll take ice tea," he said.

"Make that two, please," I chimed in.

"This restaurant is noted for our key lime pie. May I make a suggestion that you both leave room for a slice?"

"How about I wait to see if I finish my steak," said my father.

"What about you, young lady?"

"I'm getting married and have a wedding dress to get into, so I'll pass this time but thanks."

She was about to leave our table when a man from the kitchen yelled for her to come here. She excused herself and made a quick turn and headed to where he was standing. I looked at dad and he looked at me. I leaned over to whisper to my father, but I saw one of the other workers watching me. "Dad, I think I'm going to the to the ladies room to wash my hands."

"Great idea, wait for me."

We returned to find some ice cold tea waiting for us. While sitting and waiting for our meal, another waitress came to the table with a basket of rolls.

"Where is Emily?" I asked kindly.

"She had a family emergency and had to leave, so I'll be waiting on you from now on. My name is Cathy and I'll go to the kitchen to check on your food."

"Thanks," I said.

I started looking around and my eyes fell in the direction of the kitchen door. I looked again and saw Emily sitting in the last booth, near the kitchen. I saw her wipe her eyes. I pointed her out to my father and told him I would be right back.

I went over to her. When I reached her booth, she was silently wiping her eyes and sniffing.

"Emily, what's wrong?" I asked.

"Nothing."

"Maybe I should start again. Hello my name is Linda Smith and I live in Jacksonville."

"You said you were getting married. Is that why you are here?" Emily said softly.

"Yes to find a wedding dress. My father came alone to help assist me."

"Where is your mother?"

"She is facing a family crisis so she didn't come with us."

"I understand that. My mother died when I was fifteen years old," said Emily. "I was first placed in a foster home but that didn't work. Then my mother's stepsister decided to take me in. The man who yelled at me is my uncle. He hates that he had to raise me along with his four children. I have to work at this restaurant after school. He treats me terrible. I don't have anywhere else to go so I have to stay here until I'm old enough to make it on my own."

Her beautiful blue eyes were now blue and red from crying. Her face was red as a beet. She didn't look like the happy waitress who came to our table smiling just a little while ago.

"Emily, do you believe in prayer?"

"Sure do, my mother use to pray with me nightly on my knees, but when she got too weak from cancer she no longer could get down there."

I immediately started to smile. She looked up at me with an inquisitive expression on her face.

"Why are you smiling?" she wondered aloud.

"Because I was raised by an elderly couple and the lady taught me to pray on my knees. For some reason I think God does hear you better."

"I still pray on mine but looks like he has turned his back on me," she said.

"Emily, don't ever say that. Satan wants you to feel defeated, but remember we go through trials and tribulations only to make us strong."

"You mean it's nothing I've done to deserve such cruel treatment?"

"Nothing; Honey this is a part of life. I promise if you keep your hands in the Master's hand you will make it."

"I make good grades in school," Emily said. "In fact, I've been awarded academic scholarships. I plan to go to college and make something out of myself."

"Emily, keep on looking up and stay focused on God and your dreams. I promise you he will direct your path. You seem like a very nice young lady and I'm so happy I met you."

"I'm happy we talked, too," she smiled. "I'm going into the ladies room to wash my face. I intend to hold my head up high and go into that kitchen and wash those dishes."

"Is that why you were crying?"

"Yes, his own son doesn't want to do the dishes so he makes me stop waiting tables to do dishes. You have made me feel better, now I don't mind doing the dishes. I will keep telling myself it's only for a short time. I'll be at college soon."

"That a girl and Emily, when you feel depressed remember these scriptures. Emily gave me a napkin to write the scriptures down for her. I promise they will help you."

"Wait a minute, I'm going to the office to get some paper," she said. "I plan on keeping these scriptures to help me through this situation."

I patiently waited and she finally came back to the booth with a washed face and a piece of paper in her hand.

"Okay, give them to me and I'll write them down."

"I'll give you some that I remember have helped me," I told her. "Read John 14:27, James 1:5, Psalm 27:14 and Psalm 46 in its entirety. I promise you, if you spend some quality time with God he will direct your path."

"Linda, thank you. I'm so happy you came into this restaurant. I needed this. I promise to study my Bible often and keep God as the head of my life."

"Emily, I will remember you in my prayers and I want you to please remember me."

I stood to go back to my food and Emily stood and gave me a big hug. "God bless you Linda."

"Thanks Emily, may God bless you, too."

Dad was looking in my direction. As I made my way back to the table, he was smiling.

"Linda, you are something else, your salad has been on the table for a while, but I refused to interrupt you."

"Dad, you know, every where you go, you can find someone hungry for the word of God. I'm so happy that I allow the word to live in me and I'm willing to share God with others."

Dad said the grace and we ate our salads and bread together. The waitress came back to the table. This time she had two cups of hot chowder.

"Emily wanted you to have these," the waitress announced. "She said since you didn't want the potato, you might want some great chowder."

"Please tell her thanks."

Dad did some small talk between bites about his company, but I really wasn't paying much attention. My mind was on my mother. I really do miss her and wish she would either call me or let me come to see her. I was about to find some idle conversation to talk to my dad about, other than his job, when he said, "Linda, tell me about your mother? I know you said she is married and right now is having some problems. Is there anything I can help her with?"

"No, I think she has to figure this one out herself. I had a little sister named Ann. She was hit by a car in 1988 and later died. Mom was so upset about the accident that she started drinking and just let herself go. Well, she later was arrested for drinking and driving. I was about to be awarded to the state of Florida, when Mrs. Carrie and Mr. Mack Oswell became my legal guardian."

Dad placed his fork down and listened to every word I was saying. He had such a sad look on his face, but he didn't say a word. He just sat and watched me try to get the story out to him.

"Mother was not herself. She would get drunk, and start to accuse me of not watching Ann and therefore causing her untimely death. I had to go through my college years feeling unloved by her. The Oswells did all they could to make life happy for me. They became my parents. They are the very reason I went to college and graduated with honors. Dad, I tell you I owe my life to them."

"Honey, I am so sorry I wasn't there to ease the pain you went through. Like I said, I wanted so much to know where you were. All I knew is that I had a child somewhere in this big, old world and I wanted to be a part of your life."

He dropped his head and the tears started to flow down his face. I looked at him and started to cry, too. The waitress returned to our table with our food. Dad and I wiped our eyes and smiled at each other.

Dad complimented on how well his steak tasted. I immediately cut a small piece of mine and thought the same thing. My steak was tender and flavorful. I looked at my father and imagined my mother was sitting next to him. What a perfect life I could have had with him being my father and mom being a real mother to me.

The food was delicious and we both were stuffed when the waitress came over holding a large piece of key lime pie.

"Before either one of you say a word, blame in on Emily," explained the waitress. "She paid for it before she left for the day."

"When you see her again, please tell her thanks and I will keep her in my prayers.

My father and I shared the pie and had another round of ice tea. We both were full and he was worried about me driving back alone with a full stomach. I reminded him that I was only a few miles from home. He was the one who had to drive the farthest.

Dad paid the bill and excused himself from the table. I patiently waited for his return. We walked back to our cars together when he reached into his top pocket and gave me an envelope.

"What is this?" I asked.

"You may open it now or wait until you get back to Atlanta."

Curiosity got the best of me so I ripped the envelope right open. My eyes grew larger than golf balls. I was holding a ten thousand dollar check in my hand. I almost lost my lunch.

"Dad, what is this for?"

"It is for my daughter's wedding."

"But you just paid for all the dresses, including mother's entire outfit."

"Baby, I have nothing else to do with my money, and I'm just so thankful that God allowed me to live to see this day. Like I said, I can't make up for lost time, but I'm sure going to enjoy the time God gives us together. Now take this check and have one of the most beautiful weddings Atlanta has seen in a long time."

I rushed over and hugged and kissed him on the cheek. This was one of the best days I had in a long time. I was thinking, I cannot wait to call Brandon and tell him.

I told dad to please drive safely and that I would call him about six o'clock tonight. I thanked him again for everything and most of all for being with me and seeing me in my wedding dress.

He kept saying it was nothing and he was just proud to be with me during such an important occasion.

We both got into our cars and waved good bye. As I turned on to the interstate, I smiled to myself and looked from the road to the sky and said, "Thank you God for this day."

Chapter Eighteen

The ride back to Jacksonville was a happy one. My mind was on how joyous my father had made me in our short time together so far. It wasn't his money it was the quality time he had spent with me. I admired how his eyes lit up the moment I tried on the last wedding dress. He made me feel like I was a queen marrying a prince. All I needed now in my life was my mother to open her door to her house and her heart to me. I needed to let her know that I was so sorry for what I said. I was only trying to put some questions in her head. She really doesn't know Paul. In fact, if she hadn't been so taken with him, she would have figured out the same night how strange I was acting. A wise mother would have sensed the tension between Paul and me.

I decided to pop in my James Cleveland tape and listen to his *Sitting on the Banks of the Jordan*. That is one of my favorite tapes. It makes me think of Mrs. Carrie in heaven waiting on me. I miss that old lady so much, but I'm so grateful to God for placing her in my life.

I was about to get off the interstate and head to my mother's house when I looked up and found that I was closer to Monica's house. I said to myself, "I'll call her in the morning to let her know I'm on my way to her house. If I get her answering machine I'll tell her either to open the door and get her new dress or she can look out and find it hanging on the front door."

I pulled up and Monica's car was parked in front. She must have been looking out because she ran to greet me in the driveway.

"Hey, girl, come on inside and tell me all about your day with Daddy dearest," Monica said.

"Monica, help me get my mother's shoes and purse. I'll get the garment bag."

"You mean, you bought your mother a dress for the wedding?"

"Girl, I got her everything. All she has to do is show up."

"Did you find something for your bridesmaids to wear?"

"Girl, you are so crazy. I ordered your dress and it will be shipped to you in about two weeks. The sales lady will also include a scrap of material so you can get your shoes dyed the same color."

"Go girl, come on and tell me all about it and your dress, too," Monica urged.

We walked inside and I hung mother's dress up and rushed to get out of my shoes. I came back into the living room to find - what else - a large bowl of hot buttered popcorn.

"Linda, do you want any popcorn?"

"No, thank you, I recently ate."

"Okay, tell me all about your day with dad."

"Dad patiently waited for me to pick out everything for my mother. He liked your dress and, girl, when it was time for me to try on my own gown, he was there. I was happy and nervous at the same time. I slowly walked out to where he was standing. He looked up and I tell you, he opened his mouth so wide that he almost lost his dentures."

Monica started laughing so hard. She threw her hands up in the air. "Lost his dentures, now that's a good one."

"While standing there, the young lady helped me to put on my head piece. I turned and looked in the mirror and just smiled at how beautiful I looked. All I needed was Brandon standing at the other end of the store waiting for me. My father had tears in his eyes. Girl, the scene was priceless. I tell you all I needed was my mother with me."

"So, I take it he approved of everything you picked," commented Monica.

"Approved? Girl, he paid for it all! Wait right here, let me reach in my purse and show you what else he gave me."

I rushed to my purse and took the check out of the envelope and showed it to Monica.

"Wow, Linda, this check is for ten thousand dollars!"

"Monica, you can read."

"Linda, this will pay for your entire wedding and reception, too."

"Tell me about it and if I play my cards right, honeymoon, too," I said giddily.

"Girl, I need to make a copy of this and show this to my dad and ask him doesn't he want me to have this kind of a wedding. He will probably say yes, now go and ask your mother to give you the other nine thousand."

"Monica, you're so crazy. You know your father will give you what he can afford. Plus, it is not about the money. It's about being happy."

"Well, if my dad gives me ten thousand dollars, I'll be very happy, with or without Eric."

"Now, let's get down to business. Have you heard from Fred yet?" I wanted to know.

"No, I came home and checked my answering machine and nothing from Fred."

"I think I'm going to make a reservation for Friday. If I don't hear from him, I'm still going to cut my losses with my mother and head home. This has been a rewarding trip after all. I met my father and his mother. I got our dresses for the wedding, mother's dress and accessories. I had a talk with some of the neighbors and other than mother this has been a good trip."

"Speaking of your mother, how in the world are you going to give her the dress when she won't even open the door for you?"

"Good question, Monica. I'll call her in the morning and if she doesn't answer, then I'll tell her I'm leaving it hanging on her front door."

"You think she still won't talk to you?"

"I don't know. But I will start out the conversation apologizing to her and it is up to her to accept or reject it. She has really blown this out of proportion. I think she's really angry with Paul and taking it out on me."

"All I got to say is, girl, you do what you have to do and if it means going back to Atlanta without her seeing you, then so be it."

"I think I'm going into your guest room to call Brandon. I miss him so much. I want to tell him all about my day with my dad. I also want to tell him that I'm making a reservation to come home Friday."

I left Monica in the living room turning on the television. She loves her Lifetime movies. I went into the kitchen for a glass of cold water. I looked in the refrigerator and was shocked. Monica had gone grocery shopping. I was about to say, do I have the wrong house but I refused to put her on the spot.

I dialed Brandon and the answering machine picked up. It was still good hearing his voice, but I wanted to talk to him. He was probably on evening duties. Maybe I'll try in an hour to see if just maybe he was working overtime.

I took my Bible off the night stand and flipped it to Philippians 4:6,7: "*Be careful for nothing; but in every thing by prayer and supplication with thanksgiving let your requests be made known unto God. And the peace of God, which passeth all understanding, shall keep your hearts and minds through Christ Jesus.*"

I flipped the Bible to another one of my favorite chapters. Jeremiah 17:8: "*For he shall be as a tree planted by the waters, and that spreadeth out her roots by the river, and shall not see when heat cometh, but her leaf shall be green; and shall not be careful in the year of drought, neither shall cease from yielding fruit.*" When I'm worried, Philippians and Jeremiah are my scriptures of strength.

I tried calling Brandon again. This time he answered. "Hey, baby, how did things go with you and your father?"

"Oh, Brandon, I couldn't have asked for a more beautiful day. I got all the dresses, even mother's. My father paid for them all and took me out to dinner. I tell you we had the time of our lives. Oh, guess what? He gave me a check to cover my entire wedding and reception."

"He did what?"

"You heard me, he gave me a ten thousand dollar check."

"Wow, he is happy to have you in his life."

"You can say that again, and it's not just the money. I'm happy to have him in my life. Brandon, I tell you if my mother was with us today I think this would have been perfect. He asked about her again. He still loves her. I told him all about Ann's death and mother's drinking problem. He looked as if he wished he were with her during that ordeal. I'm so happy I found him and I know he feels the same way about me."

"Linda, I'm so happy for you and believe me if someone deserves to be happy, that someone is you. I miss you so much; when are you coming back home?"

"Funny you asked. I was just telling Monica that I was going to call the airlines to make a reservation to leave here Friday."

"That means I have three more days to be alone."

"Brandon, you aren't alone. You have patients to keep you busy."

"Yes, but I can't tell them how much I love them."

"Brandon, you're making me blush. I'm getting off this phone so I can call my father to thank him for today and the money."

"Okay. I'll be waiting to hear from you Thursday, so I can pick you up from the airport. Good night, my love."

"Good night, Brandon, and I love you too."

I was all smiles when I placed that phone on the hook. I wanted to scream to the top of my lungs how much I loved that man. Instead, I just smiled and said, "Thank you God for giving me Brandon."

I went back into the living room to find Monica asleep, and the Lifetime movie looking at her. I quietly turned off the television and headed back into the guest room to call my father.

"Dad, I just wanted to call and thank you for today and the money."

"Oh, Linda. Like, I said, it was a pleasure being with you. I had a great time and if the check I gave you isn't enough, just call me and I'll next day air you more."

"Dad thanks, but this is more than enough. In fact, I'll probably have some left to take on our honeymoon."

"Linda, all I want is for you to be happy. Please don't worry about anything. Just know that I'm here for you and your mother, if she needs me too."

Chapter Nineteen

I rolled over and looked at the clock to find it was eight o'clock. I must have been one tired lady. I rushed into the bath to freshen up because I had plans to call my mother to tell her I was on my way there to bring her the dress and come for a visit.

When I got out of the bathroom, the phone was ringing. I wasn't about to get it, but then I heard the voice of Fred.

"Fred, this is Linda."

"Linda, what are you doing at Monica's?"

"Long story, but short version, my mother and me had a falling out. I left her house, moved into a hotel, the kitchen caught on fire, so now I'm staying here with Monica until Friday."

"Well, I'm happy I caught you. I have completed my investigation and want to know when you can come by to see me."

"I was about to call my mother to take her a gift. Then I'm free for the rest of the day."

"Well, I have a meeting outside the city limits this afternoon. Can you be at my office at ten o'clock and go by your mother's afterward."

"I sure can, so I'll see you at ten. Hey Fred, thanks."

I hung up that phone nervous and happy at the same time. He never said what he found, so I really don't know if he found anything. I just don't know. I'm dialed my mother to tell her I'll be over to visit her this afternoon.

"Hello, mother, this is Linda, how are you?"

"Linda, how do you think I am?"

"Mother, I didn't call to argue. I called to apologize to you. If I said anything to offend you, please forgive me. I have your best interest in heart. Now, listen, before you hang up. I went shopping for my wedding dress and found the dress, shoes and purse for you. I have a meeting this morning and I would like to bring it by your house this afternoon for you."

"Linda, that is nice, but I really don't feel like company."

"Mother, I promise not to stay…"

I hung up the phone feeling like a motherless child. I sat down and the tears started to flow down my cheek. I cried and cried. "Lord, how long will my mother treat me like this? All I ever wanted was for her to love me. She fooled me when I was in the hospital sick. She told me that she thought she was about to lose me. Yeah, right, once again she is proving her love for me."

I got up and went to the bathroom to wash my face. I knew that I had an appointment with Fred and this was one I was keeping.

Monica's phone started to ring. I looked at it, but knew not to answer it. The machine picked up and I could clearly hear Monica's voice, "Linda, are you there? This is Monica. Pick up."

"Monica, I'm still here. What do you want?"

"I wanted to see if you can meet me downtown for lunch today?"

"No. Fred called and I'm going to take my mother her things."

"Girl, did I hear you said Fred called?"

"You heard me! I'm trying to get myself ready to meet him."

"Do you want me to come along, or do you feel you can handle this?"

"I'm going to get ready, spend a little time in prayer and then go to his office. I'm a little scared, but then I might as well get this behind me. Like it or not, I'm making my plane reservation today and will leave here Friday. I think I've been here long enough."

"Okay, but you have my work number and if you need me for support, just call."

"I will and, hey, Monica, thanks for being such a dear friend."

"Hey, I'm not only being a friend, I want to know if Fred found any dirt on Mr. Paul."

"Monica, just when I think you are serious, you say something stupid. See you later."

I went into my room and knelt down for a word of prayer. "Dear Heavenly Father, first of all I want to thank you for this day. I want to thank you for saving my soul, and most of all for dying on the cross for my sins.

Now, Lord, I'm going to see Fred. I'm a little afraid of what I might find. I want to help clear the young girl's good name. Lord, I can't lie to you. I want Paul to get his just due for what he tried to do to me. Lord, please forgive me. I'm talking from the flesh and not my spirit. I know my mother loves this man, so I'm asking for you to fix her heart, so that if I find some disturbing news, she will be able to handle it. One more request: Lord please let my mother love me again. Even though she has mistreated me, I've always loved her. Lord, I thank you for all the blessings you have given me and I know my 'faith holds the key' to you unlocking and answering all my problems."

The drive to Fred's office was one of prayer and meditation. I asked God to be in the mist of this. I wanted to know if he had some helpful information or not. I kept trying to calm myself down, but to no avail. I was driving and talking to the Lord the entire way to Fred's office.

I pulled into the nearest parking space and slowly made my way to the building. My knees were shaking, my heart beating so fast, and the palm of my hands were sweating.

As I touched the outer door knob, I noticed it was warm from the sun. As I opened the entry door a gush of cold air blew across my face. I took a deep breath. Then, I whispered, "Lord here we go."

"May I help you please?"

"Yes, I'm… I'm here to see Fred."

"Is he expecting you?"

I wanted to say no, I've changed my mind, but then I would still owe him for all the trouble he has gone through. "Yes, he's expecting me. Please tell him Linda Smith is here."

"Please have a seat and I'll buzz him now and let him know you are here."

The door flew open and Fred came into the lobby.

"Linda, thank you for coming; sorry you had to change your appointment."

"It's no problem. Like I said, I'll make my other appointment after I leave here."

I followed him into his tidy office. He sat in his padded chair and said, "Now first of all, I want you to take a look at this picture and tell me if this is Paul Lawrence Richmond."

My hand was actually shaking while reaching for the picture. I almost lost it when I saw it was Paul. He was standing in my mother's front yard.

"Yes, that is him."

"Good. Then we have the correct person."

I swallowed, took a deep breath and waited for Fred to carry this conversation forward.

"Linda, I'm sorry it has taken me a while, but I had to go out of town to question some of Paul's old neighbors. I've found out some chilling information about this man. Are you sure you are ready for what I've found?"

"Yes. That is why I hired you to tell me all about this man."

"I took the liberty of highlighting the important part of his profile. I did include information about where he was born, parent's name, siblings, and high school, college, and military records. I did find out that he doesn't have any biological children. I also found out that he was married to Martha Clark. They were married for eighteen years."

"He said he was married to a lady for that long, but she died of cancer," I interjected.

"Linda, please let me finish. The news he told you was half truth. His wife died of depression. She gave up the will to live. What I am saying is Paul killed her."

"He did what?" I found myself now standing in the middle of the floor looking down at Fred. My face felt flushed and I was about to burst. I said he did what?"

"Linda, if we are going to get to the end of this, you will have to stay seated. I promise to give you this folder containing all the information I was able to find."

"Fred, I will not interrupt again, but this is making my blood boil. I'm thinking if he lied about this, then what else has he not told the truth about."

"Good question. He used to live in Charleston, South Carolina, until he was accused of fondling a teenage girl in the neighborhood. This girl tried to get her parents to believe her, but since she was a troubled teen, no one believed her. Paul and Martha moved to Macon, Georgia. They stayed there until Paul was accused of doing the same thing. This time he was arrested and was about to be sentenced to prison, when he plea bargained."

"Fred, I'm confused. If he plea-bargained, then he didn't do any time. How did you find out this information?"

"Linda, I'm a single man. I have nothing to do, but to put my heart and soul in my work. I'm one of the best investigators money can buy. I have ways of uncovering all kinds of dirt on people. I can't tell you the tricks of the trade, but what I can tell you is the second time Paul was accused, his wife was so humiliated, she fell into a deep depression and later died. "

"Fred, what you are saying is he inadvertently caused her death. My mother is acting the same way; she sit and stares into space for hours. I refuse to sit by and let this happen to her. I have another question. Did the judge impose any restrictions, such as revoking his license and forbidding his influence on teenage girls?"

"I did find out the judge ordered him to see a therapist."

"Did he? Did you find out the therapist's name? Did you talk to the therapist?"

"Linda, I didn't find out if he did or not. But I do know that after his wife Martha died, he drifted from place to place until he landed a job in Jacksonville. The principal was an old college friend of his. So, naturally, he offered him a job and the rest as they say is history."

"Fred, I'll take the time to read the whole file, but what you are saying is Paul has a problem with girls?"

"Yes, that is exactly what I'm saying."

"I'm taking this folder right to my mother right now! She needs to read all about what you found on her dear old Paul. I will then take this information to the school, so they will know that the girl was telling the truth."

"Linda, you seem to have a vendetta against Paul. Is there something I should know?"

"No! You have given me my money's worth and I'm going to use this information to clear this girl's good name. Paul will not get off so easy this time."

I thanked Fred for his help. I gladly wrote him a check and walked out of that office feeling like a cat that had just eaten a big fat rat. I got into the car, turned on my radio and instead of a good gospel song, there was a minister on the air preaching on the subject of sin.

I was about to pull off the lot when the preacher said, "He who is without sin cast the first stone. The lady who was caught in adultery was standing with her accusers, but when God made that statement, they all ran. There was no one standing, but her and Jesus. I tell you when you dig a ditch for one, you better dig two."

I cut the radio off, but I could still hear the preacher's voice saying, "If you dig a ditch for one, you better dig a ditch for two."

I started thinking like Mrs. Carrie. Don't do evil for evil. I should just throw the envelope in the garbage and let God handle Paul. But then, I thought, "Why pay all that money for nothing. If you don't want your mother to find out the truth, then mail it to the school board."

I pulled off the road, cut my car off and said, "Lord, I got my answer. I now know that I didn't do anything to cause Paul to attack me. He has a problem and I'm giving this to you. When I get to Monica's house,

I will destroy this and not hurt my mother. I know you will take care of Paul. He might have gotten by, but he will not get away."

I headed to my mother's house to take her things for the wedding. I started feeling better about my decision. It was like I had finally found inner peace. I turned on my gospel tape and put Paul completely out of my mind.

Chapter Twenty

I was headed in the direction of my mother's house when I noticed an ambulance coming behind me. I pulled over to wait for him to pass. I slowly pulled back on the road and made my way to my mother's house. I was about five houses down when I saw the ambulance sitting on the street near my mother's house.

I pushed on the gas to rush to the scene. As I made my way through the crowd, I saw that the ambulance was indeed parked directly in front of my mother's house. I rushed to the ambulance, but no one was inside. I was about to go into my mother's yard when the paramedics were bringing someone out. I rushed over to see who it was. It was Paul. He had an oxygen mask over his face. He looked as if he was fighting to breathe.

My mother was the last to exit her house. She was yelling for him to please don't leave her. I ran to hold her in my arms. She looked at me and said in a loud voice, "I told you this thing was killing him, but you thought it wasn't. Paul holds things inside and you see what it is doing to him. Now get out of my way so I can go to the hospital with him!"

I moved to the side, feeling so low. I wish I had never come to Jacksonville. Mom's door was wide open. One of the neighbors said she would lock up, but I asked her to wait and let me bring in a garment bag and two other items I had purchased for my mother.

I laid the garment bag across the living room couch and placed the shoes and handbag in the chair. I wrote mother a note. Dear mother, I am so sorry for all the pain I've caused you, I pray you will find it in your heart to forgive me. I want you at my wedding. I love you very much, your only child, Linda.

I sat there a few minutes and looked around the house, it was clean and, I mean, a little too clean. There wasn't a smell of food in the air. I went into the kitchen and there were no leftover containers in the refrigerator. I thought to myself: *what are they eating these days*? I did however notice how frail my mother was looking. I could clearly see she had lost some weight. I was about to go into the bedroom when a neighbor came into the house.

"Linda, I promised Vivian I would lock up, so if you don't mind, I'm ready to do just that."

"Yes, I'm ready to leave."

I slowly headed to the front door, but not before taking one last look. I was thinking what will happen to my mother if Paul dies?

I rushed to my car to head back to Monica's house. I wanted so badly to go to the hospital to be with my mother but I didn't want to upset her anymore. When I got to Monica's house, she was still at work. The light was flashing on her answering machine. Something inside of me said to push the button and I did.

"Linda, this is Monica, I'm so sorry, but I have to work a few hours over, but I'll be straight home so we can talk. If you need me just call me. You have my work number."

I started to call her just and tell her that I would leave her keys under her mattress because I would be flying back to Atlanta. I wanted to get out of Jacksonville. I was feeling lonely and needed to see Brandon.

I sat there thinking about Paul's condition and how this was affecting my mother. I felt so sorry for the both of them. I wanted to call the hospital, but I was sure they would not give me any information on his condition.

I called the airlines and made a reservation. The lady said there was a flight leaving Jacksonville in three hours. I told her to book that flight for me. I gathered my things and placed Monica's keys under her mattress and made my way to the airport. My plans were to turn in the rental car, call Monica and leave a message on her answering machine. I would thank her for the hospitality she showed me, but it was time to go home.

I had plenty of time after checking in, so I called Monica and thanked her for being there for me. I also called Brandon and gave him my flight number and time of my arrival.

As I sat there I had nothing to do, but think about my mother. I couldn't get her demeanor out of my mind. Instead of her wanting me with her, she treated me like I was a total stranger.

I had to make one last call and that was to my father. I knew he would be happy to hear from me.

"Dad, this is Linda. How are you?"

"Linda, it is good hearing your voice. You sound funny. Is everything okay?"

"No, I'm leaving Jacksonville and just wanted to let you know that if you want to reach me, I'll be back in Atlanta. I was supposed to leave Friday, but I decided to leave today. I want to thank you for making my trip wonderful and I thank God we got together."

"Honey, I thank God that you found me. Like I said we will never be separated again. I'm also very happy that you got a chance to meet my mother. I've been to visit her today and all she talked about making it to your wedding. I am going to hire a nurse to come with us, so please, when you get settled send me some hotel information."

"Dad, I have a condo, you and grandmother are more than welcome to stay with me."

"I know, honey, but mother will need wheelchair accessibility and I think a hotel would be more convenient."

"Well, dad it's time for me to board my flight. I just wanted to say hello and, again, thanks for everything."

"Linda, thank you and call me when your flight lands."

"I will. See you dad."

"Bye baby."

It was a quick and smooth flight. I was so happy to be back in Atlanta. I got off and was headed for my luggage. I walked and looked at the people waiting for their loved ones. I was looking for Brandon. I took the escalator down and as I got level to the floor, I couldn't help but notice a handsome man standing with his arms full of mixed-colored, long stem roses. I ran straight to Brandon's waiting arm.

"Brandon, I missed you and I feel like I have been gone for a month."

"Come here and give me a kiss. It does seem as if you've been gone forever. I tell you this is the last trip without me.

Hey, you surprised me. What are you doing home so soon?"

"When we get to the car, we have a lot to talk about."

I looked up and said in a soft whisper, "Thank you God. I'm home again."

I told Brandon to just listen. Because so much has happened to me in such a short time that it's going to take weeks for me to tell him everything. He reminded me that I did tell him about my mother and having a falling out with her. He also reminded me that I told him about the fire, Fred, the private investigator, and all the wedding plans.

"Brandon, I forgot to tell you that I took my mother her dress and accessories for the wedding. When I got on her street, I noticed an ambulance and it was for Paul. I think he was having a heart attack. I know they had the oxygen mask over his face."

"Linda, do you think he is going to be alright?"

"I think so, but I wanted to stay and be a support for my mother, but when she saw me she lost it again. I tell you she is so upset at him. But she needed someone to lash out at and that someone was me! I decided to cut my losses and head back here to you. I needed to feel loved and I know you love me."

"You can say that again, and I'm very much in love with you. Hey, what did you find out from Fred?"

"I have the folder in my luggage. I think it would better if you to read it for yourself. I tell you that man has a problem, but I decided not to show it to my mother. I am just going to let God handle Paul."

"Linda, I have no comment. You needed to know who he was and now you do. All I can say is I'm so happy you are back home with me. Now, we can work on the rest of our wedding plans together."

"Yes, we can. I've thought about several places to host the reception, but we can look at them together."

Brandon helped me with all of my luggage, and he insisted on ordering a pizza so we could sit and talk for a few hours. Just as the pizza arrived and he took a few bites, he was summoned to the hospital.

"Linda, this is one thing you will have to get used to: me being called away at any given moment."

"Brandon, you go on and take a few slices of pizza to eat on the way. I'll eat a few and put the rest up for another time. I'm kind of tired anyway, so we can talk tomorrow."

"Yes, and Linda, it sure is good having you home."

"Brandon it's good being home, too."

"Good morning Holy Spirit" what a good feeling waking up in my own bed. I refuse to leave this house until I clean it from top to bottom. However, before I do anything I need to go through the large pile of mail I have on my desk. I also need to pay a few bills then make some important calls.

First things first, I must call Monica. I know she is on pins and needles wanting to know all about Paul.

"Hello Monica, this is Linda. How are you?"

"I know who you are, and I'm about to kill you. Why didn't you call me last night?"

"Monica, to tell you the truth, I needed to spend a little time with Brandon. We sat up and talked for awhile until he was paged to go back to the hospital. I then took a long hot shower and went to bed. When I got up this morning, you were one of the people I had on my mind."

"Yeah, right, you know I want to know all about Paul."

"Monica, I found out he had been accused of touching other girls in the past, so I know he has a problem."

"So does this mean you are going to tell your mother?"

"No, I've decided to let God handle Paul."

"So what about all the money you spent on this investigation?"

"It does not matter. I got my answer and now I'm going to destroy this file."

"Well, Linda, it's your money. Do as you please!"

"Monica, now don't be angry with me. I've searched my heart and this is what I decided to do. Case closed!"

"Okay, now what?"

"What! I'm going to make some calls so Brandon and I can start looking for a place to host our wedding reception. This thing with Paul is over. Please be my friend and give it a rest."

"Okay, I'll never bring up the subject again."

"Well, I know you are at work and I just wanted you to know what was going on. Thanks again for letting me stay at your house. Oh, I take it you found the key under your mattress."

"Yes, and you are always welcome at my house."

"Thanks, and you have a good day. Bye."

I decided not to go through my mail just now. My mind was really on getting my small journal out and writing my notes, placing it in my Bible and locking it up. I went to my small lock box and opened it to reread my old notes.

1. Will Paul get his just due for what he tried to do to me?
2. Will I meet my biological father?
3. If so, will he accept or reject me.

I walked over to the dinning room table to have a comfortable seat. I wanted to add to my list.

4. Will my mother ever forgive me and come to my wedding?
5. Will Brandon's mother finally accept me as her daughter-in-law?

I didn't want to add any more of my worries, so I shut the book, placed it back on top of my Bible, and locked it up in my lock box.

"Lord, I know that I have faith that you hold the key to unlocking my problems, and I feel if I continue to trust you, you will answer my problems. I feel in my heart that whatever comes out of my life situation is supposed to be, because you are the head of my life."

I placed the box back on the shelf in the top of my closet and went back into the dining room to open and read my long awaited pile of bills, junk mail, magazines, and old papers.

I sorted through the mess and was about to take a ride to my old job when the phone rang. It was my supervisor. He said he took a gamble on calling me since he heard that I was in Florida on personal business. He wanted to know how I was doing and if I was still returning to work next week. I had to remind him that I was still under the doctor's care and I was really supposed to be off two more weeks. I told him I would call the doctor and set up an appointment Monday. If the doctor says so, I'll return to work Tuesday.

He said he had a project and needed my help. He made me feel needed. He said it was budget time and reminded me no one can crunch those numbers like the two of us. I laughed so hard it really made me feel like old times. I told him I could work the extra hours, but no junk food for me, please, I have a wedding dress to get into. I ended the conversation by telling him I would call him or see him on Tuesday.

I got my purse and rushed out of the door before someone else called. I felt like a manicure and pedicure. I wanted to go to the same health spa my future sister-in-law Lynda had introduced me to. But I decided to go to one in the mall. I would wait and go to Essentials, the day spa, when Lynda comes for the wedding. This time, I would be the one to treat her. I found myself actually smiling at myself when I thought about how much fun we had together.

Chapter Twenty One

On the ride home, while stopped for a red light, I couldn't help, but notice what a great job the lady had done on my hands. I looked down to admire my feet. Then the motorist behind me started blowing his horn. I said to myself, "Everyone is in such a hurry these days."

I was changing lanes when I noticed a small shopping center. Just as I swung into the parking lot my eyes fixed on the small bridal shop. I rushed into the store just to see what they had. A lady came from the back of the store to greet me.

"May I help you please?'

"Yes, I'm getting married in September and would like to see some of your wedding invitations."

I followed her to the back of the store and sat down at one of the many tables. She brought me a stack of books and asked if I knew the style or color I was looking for. I told her no, I had time and I would just go through all of the books, if necessary. She looked at me as if she didn't have all the time in the world, so hurry up.

I flipped through all the books, yet nothing caught my eye. There was a stack of papers nearby, so I started jotting down ideas for my wedding invitations. I took a sheet and wrote, "Vivian Smith and Alphonso Banks request the honor of your presence at the marriage of their daughter, Linda Nicole Smith, to Dr. Brandon Alexander." Oh my God, I don't know Brandon's middle name. Here I'm marrying a man and don't even know his middle name. I got so tickled that I almost fell out of the chair.

The sales lady came to my rescue and wanted to know what was so funny. I told her I was marrying a man and didn't know his middle name. She said there have been people in here that knew less about their future spouses than you do, so just go home and ask him before purchasing the invitations.

I left there with some ideas as to how I wanted my invitations to look, but I dared not purchase them without Brandon being with me.

I stopped by for a Chinese carryout meal. I'd had a full day and was starting to feel a little tired. I was in no shape to prepare dinner. I thought about the pizza, but I'll put that in the freezer for another day. All I wanted was for Brandon to come by and we share a takeout candle light dinner for two.

I arrived home to find everything as I'd left it. There were a pile of papers on the dining room table and the trash can was full of unwanted mail. I rushed to clean off the table so the room could look nice. Tonight Brandon and I are having Chinese by candlelight.

I put the nice, new, white-lace tablecloth with matching cloth place mats on the table. I looked in the drawer to locate my crystal candleholders. Along side the holders were the unused, long, pink candles. I made the napkins stand in the middle of the mats to look like the ones in my Good Housekeeping magazine.

In the middle of the table there already sat a flower arrangement consisting of beautiful, silk, pink, red and white roses. I smiled to myself thinking that when Brandon comes to dinner, he will believe that I've been working all day to make this a great dinner. Seeing that it had been a while since we've had a nice, home-cooked dinner together, I really should have taken the time to prepare one, but not tonight. I'll be his wife soon and will be cooking every night. I looked at the clock and it was now 5.

I reached for the phone to call Brandon. When I looked at the answering machine, there was no flashing light, a definite indication I didn't have any phone messeges. I was just about to make the call when the phone started to ring.

"Hello"

"Linda, I'm calling to say I won't be able to make it to dinner tonight. One of the doctors here asked me to stay and keep an eye on his patient. He is too tired and I told him I would cover for him. I know you have gone to a lot of trouble and this is our first dinner together in a long time. I promise I will make it up to you tomorrow. I will even pretend the leftovers are a freshly prepared gourmet meal."

"Brandon, like you said, if I am going to be your wife, I will have to get used to this. Don't worry about dinner. We can have something new tomorrow. I'll just eat a little, take a shower and catch up on my reading. Call me in the morning."

"Okay, and Linda, I love you."

"I love you, too, and I'll see you tomorrow."

I hung up the phone and did just as I'd said. I left the table all dressed for dinner tomorrow night. I went into the kitchen to prepare a plate of food then headed off to the living room to eat while watching whatever was on television.

Nothing of interest was on TV so I turned it off, finished eating and headed to the kitchen to clean up my dishes. I put the rest of the leftovers in zip lock bags for dinner another day.

I took a nice hot shower and was then ready for bed. I got on my knees to have a little talk with Jesus: "Lord here I am again. It's like the old saying, 'It's not my mother, not my father, but its me old Lord standing in the need of prayer.' Lord, I thank you for all you have done for me. You have brought me from a mighty, long way and for that I'm grateful. Lord, when I look over my life, see how far you have brought me I can just scream, thank you Jesus! Lord, I'm so worried about my mother. She has put her life in Paul's hands and she really doesn't know all about him, but I didn't get down here to talk about her. All I can say is to please bless her and open her eyes. Lord, you said in the Bible it is better to put trust in you than in man and that is what I am praying for: my mother to have trust in you and not man. Lord, I thank you for bringing me home again and keeping me safe. Lord, I pray that I'm well enough to return to work. Lord, I know I'm healed because you don't half- heal anyone. You heal them all the way. Lord, thank you for everything and most of all dying on the cross for my sins. These and other blessings I ask in your name. Amen."

The doctor gave me a clean bill of health and I felt excited about that. I pulled into the parking lot of AMX Electronics. My stomach was felt like I'd had butterflies for breakfast. I could actually feel each beat of my heart hitting against my chest. I took a deep breath and said, "Now Lord, you gave me this job and I know it has been a few months since I've been here. Please give me strength. I know these people and I know my job. I also know you did not give me the spirit of fear. Lord, you said in 2 Timothy 1:7, *For God hath not given us the spirit of fear; but of power, and of love, and of a sound mind.* I know I can make it with you on my side." I took a deep breath and headed for the front door.

"Welcome back, Linda."

I walked in and all of the front office staff was standing in the aisle waiting for me. I could actually feel tears welling up in my eyes.

"Hello everyone; it is good to be back."

Marvin, the head of the company, made his way towards me.

"You said you would call me Monday and when I didn't get a call, I figured the doctor didn't release you."

"Marvin, I wanted to quietly come back but a little bird must have told you I was coming back today, so you must have spread the word because you guys have cake and lots of goodies."

Before I could thank everyone, someone from the back yelled speech, speech.

"Okay, I'd like to say it is good being back to work. I thank you all for the calls, flowers, money and any act of kindness that was shown to me. I especially thank you for the prayers."

Benny, the employee who keeps everyone laughing, yelled from the back of the line, "I was the one who sent the money, now I'm broke so can I have some of it back."

Everyone laughed and so did I. There were exchanges of hugs and kisses. It felt good being back at work. Marvin told me to take it slow, but I told him the doctor gave me a clean bill of health and I was ready to work. I reminded him that I was still getting married in September and was going on a nice honeymoon. He was so happy to have me back he approved my leave right there on the spot.

I went into my old office and found it looking as if I'd never been gone. Mary walked in with her usual friendly smile. She was one of the best secretaries anyone could ever ask for. She didn't mind coming in early or staying late, she almost always stayed until the job was finished.

"Welcome back, boss."

"Mary, you look well. I really missed your friendly smile and most of all your caring personality. Hey, thanks for taking care of everything in my absence. I must say you are a God-sent lady. Speaking of helping me, do you take bribes?"

"Yes, I do."

"Well, close my door and have a seat."

Mary rushed to do just as I asked. She ran back and took a seat in one of my plush guest chairs. I was fumbling in my purse as I was looking for the diamond earrings I had purchased for her. I finally pulled out the professionally wrapped box. The jewelry store had done a great job for me. Mary's eyes were large as golf balls.

"Mary, since you take bribes, I want you to have this. This is a token of my appreciation for holding down the fort while I was away."

"Oh boss, I was just doing my job, but thanks for going to all the trouble. Now, give me the gift so I can open it to see what's in there for little old me."

Mary's fingers were shaking as she ripped the paper from the box. She was smiling and showing all of her teeth. "Linda, these are for me? Now, you have gone too far this time. How can you top this when you give me my Christmas gift, or is this supposed to be for Christmas, birthday, and Favorite Employee Day?"

"Mary, you are so crazy. This is just for being so kind to me. Christmas will have to wait. I just may give you a bonus or bring you a nice gift from my honeymoon."

"Forget about the honeymoon. The bonus will do just fine. I told you I take bribes."

We both hugged and laughed. I love Mary because she has a great sense of humor. No matter what problems she has in her life, she looks at the positive. I'm blessed to have someone like her working so close to me.

She pulled her long blond hair back and asked me for a rubber band. She wanted to put the earrings on and sport them around the office. I reminded her that I didn't bring enough for the entire staff, so she better let those be a secret between the two of us.

She walked over to my bookcase and got my Bible. She placed it on the desk, held up her right hand and placed her left hand on the Bible. She said, "I, Mary Hodges, promise to not tell a soul, well, not tell any employee at AMX that my boss, Linda Smith, purchased me these diamond earrings, so help me."

I told her I believed her. Then for her to put my Bible back on the shelf and scoot. I needed to call Brandon to tell him how my day was going so far.

She rushed out and closed the door behind her. I reached for the phone when I heard a soft knock. I said to myself, "What now?"

"Boss, you have a delivery."

Mary left and returned with a large crystal vase full of the most beautiful cut of unusual, fresh flowers.

"Don't look at me, I didn't order them," she offered. "I'm just going to place them on your desk, so you can read the card."

I opened the card and just as I thought, they were from Brandon. He was wishing me a good first day back to work. I smiled as I placed the card in my desk drawer.

Mary was calling me on my speakerphone.

"What now, Mary?"

"I just wanted to say if you need anything, just call me. And boss, it is really good having you back with us."

"Thanks Mary, and guess what? It is good being back."

I called Brandon to tell him thanks for the flowers, but all I got was his answering service. I left a message anyway. No sooner had I placed the phone on the hook than I got a call from Marvin. He wanted to slowly work me back into the swing of things. I looked in my mirror to see if I looked okay and made my way to his office.

My day turned out to be very productive. Marvin and I worked closely together. He wanted to make sure I was brought up to date on what had been going on in the company. We were so busy that he ordered in lunch, so we didn't have to stop working.

Chapter Twenty Two

"Good morning Holy Spirit, I thank God for allowing me to see another day. Lord, life is good; I have my health and strength, a very nice man who I will be marrying soon, and a wonderful job."

I took my shower and got ready for work. I was feeling like a million bucks. I was about to walk out when the phone started ringing. I hesitated to answer, but something inside of me said to answer it.

"Hello"

"Linda, girl, this is Monica, how are you?"

"I'm wonderful, girl. If I was any better I'd be twins."

"Well, twin, I have some bad news. I called your mother to see how she was getting along. She said she was on her way out of town for a few weeks. She just needed to get away to think. She said she buried Paul the other day."

"Monica, please let me sit down. What did you say?"

"You heard me right. Paul is dead. Remember when you left and he was being taken to the hospital. Well, he was having chest pains and breathing problems. He never came home. I don't know the entire story. All I know is your mother got off the phone in a hurry."

"Monica, thanks I'm calling Mrs. Williams. She knows all the neighborhood gossip."

"You got that right! If you need me just call me."

"Okay, I will, and thanks again."

I couldn't find Mrs. Williams' phone number fast enough.

"Mrs. Williams, this is Linda."

"Child, I know your voice. They tell me you were here a few weeks ago and never came by to see us in this old neighborhood, how come?"

"I'm sorry, but I was home on business."

"Oh. So much business, you couldn't stop to say hello."

"Mrs. Williams, I'm sorry. Please forgive me I was wrong."

"Dead wrong if you ask me."

"Okay dead wrong. Now, I want to know if you have seen or heard from my mother?"

"No, not since Paul died. I went to pay my respect. Your mother had on a hat with a veil that covered her entire face. Some of the people said she was really mourning, while others said she was hiding from the public."

"Mrs. Williams, I heard she was leaving town for a few weeks. Do you know with whom?"

"No, probably going somewhere close. I'll ask around and call you if I find out anything."

"Thanks, I'm so worried about her."

"I bet you are. I know she isn't with anyone at that school of hers because the principal was an old college friend of Paul's and he hired him on the spot. The news is he didn't do a background check on him and now the principal's job is in jeopardy. I tell you what you do in the dark, surely comes out."

I didn't comment. I wanted to ask her what was she talking about, but I didn't want her to spill her guts anymore. Now, all I was concerned about was my mother.

"Mrs. Williams, thanks for the helpful information. I'll keep trying to reach my mother."

I couldn't get the phone hung up quick enough. Paul is dead. Wow! I hate that my mother is going though this all alone. I just wish she would stop hating me so and call me. I would rush to her side in a minute.

I needed to call Brandon with this new information about Paul and get myself to work. Nothing I could do about it then. I didn't have any knowledge of Paul's death, or where my mother was. All I could do is keep her in my prayers and ask God to direct her path.

I finally arrived at work. I had plenty to do, but my mind was on my mother. I kept whispering a silent prayer asking God to please let me hear from her.

After spending the time at work in body only, my day was finally over. I thanked God for helping me see the day through. I had my jacket in one hand and a few papers to take home in a folder in the other. I was about to push the down button when I thought I heard a faint call.

"Linda, don't you leave so quickly; I have three checks for you to please sign."

"Mary you usually beat me out of here, why are you still here?"

"I'm so busy and behind with a few assignments. I need your signature on these checks."

"Okay, I'm not walking all the way back to my locked office, so bring them to the receptionist desk and let me sign them there."

"You aren't going to take a seat and read them first? Boss you're slipping. What's on your mind anyway?"

"Mary, I have a lot on my mind. I'm worried about my mother. Give the checks to me and I'll quickly look them over before signing."

"Linda, I need to come in a little early, is that okay with you?"

"Yes, but I'm not paying overtime."

"Come on Linda, you usually do."

"Mary, I'm just kidding; take what time you need to get the work out."

"Thanks, see you in the morning."

"Yes, but it will be after nine o'clock."

I rushed home to see if I had a call on my answering machine. The light was blinking so I pushed it to hear the message. It wasn't my mother.

"Linda, this is Brandon's sister, Lynda. I just wanted you to know that the dress arrived and it fits perfectly. I will go out and get my shoes and purse dyed and I'll be ready. If you need any assistance, please call me and I'll be there to help. I'm not only talking about the wedding arrangements, but I'm willing to help finance it, too. Please call me. Love you."

Wow! I was so happy to finally hear some good news that I played the message again. I saved it to let Brandon hear it later. I thought that was the only message, when I got the shock of my life.

"Linda, you really don't know me but I'm Brandon's mother. I'm calling to let you know I am available to assist you in any way. After all, this is my son's wedding, too. Please call me. I'll be waiting to hear from you. Chow."

What happened to the word good-bye? Just when everything seemed to be going well, old Satan rears his ugly head again. "Lord how much of this can one person take? I miss my mother and now my future mother-in-law wants to be the wedding planner."

There was a knock on the front door. I was about to pretend I wasn't even home when I heard a familiar voice coming from the other side of the door. "Linda, I know you are in there. Now open this door before I kick it off the hinges!"

I rushed to the door because my neighbor, Denise, means what she says. I opened the door to find Denise standing there in a blue jeans jumpsuit. She had on matching blue jeans shoes.

"Girl, come here and give me a hug," I said. "Look at you dressed like you are on your way to a date."

"Date! I just got back in town. I went out of town on business and turned that trip into a pleasure trip. I've been all over New York. I tell you I ran from top to bottom. See, I have some old friends and relatives there, so they showed me the city. Girl, it is good having you back. When I left, I gave your key to Brandon so he could put your mail on the table."

"Yes, I found the pile of mail and it took me quite a while to go through it. I thank you so much and looks like you did a little dusting while I was away."

"Yes, I did and I will be billing you for my service. Now give me a cold soda and let's talk about your trip to Jacksonville."

While I was fixing the drinks, Denise took a seat and made herself comfortable. I walked back in with a tray of cokes. I asked her if she wanted anything to snack on. She said no. All she wanted was something cold to drink.

"Now, Linda tell me, how was your mother when you got there?"

"Do you have some time or are you in a hurry?" I asked.

"Girl, I got all the time in the world. I don't go back to work until Monday."

"Denise, my mother and I fell out again."
"You did what?"

"Now listen, you drink your coke and let me do the talking. I made the comment to my mother, what did the girl have to gain by lying on Paul? My mother got so upset she told me to leave her house and never return. I moved into a hotel. While I was there, two of my school friends came and spent the night. We had a good time. I went to Sanford and met my biological father. Denise, I tell you he is wonderful. I have his eyes, and guess what? I got to meet his mother. She asked me to forgive her for the pain she inflicted upon my mother. My father even met me at the bridal shop. He gave me a check to pay for my wedding."

"How much did he give you? I bet five thousand dollars."

"Denise, if you want me to talk about everything you will have to be quiet and listen. For the record, he gave me ten thousand."

"Ten thousand dollars? Please, tell him I'm his daughter, too."

"Denise, you are so crazy. Anyway, I was so grateful for him giving me this money and I know it will help me financially. Anyway, I hired a private investigator and he did an exceptional investigation on Paul."

"Linda, now you better give up the information. I want to know all the dirt he uncovered on Paul. I mean, don't leave anything out."

"Denise, I still have the records but I had second thoughts about letting my mother see them. I was taking her dress, shoes, and purse to her house when I noticed an ambulance in the front of her house. When I got there, I noticed it was Paul being carried out. Mother screamed at me in front of the neighbors, and at that moment I made my plans to leave Jacksonville. When I got back here, I started back to work and got a call from one of my friends that Paul died."

"He what? Girl, how is your mother handling this?"

"I don't know. You see, she never called me to tell me that Paul died, but Mrs. Williams, one of the old neighbors, said my mother left the funeral and made plans to leave Jacksonville for a few weeks. She was told that my mother wanted to go away to clear her head. I wish she would have called me. I would have flown there for the funeral and brought her back here to rest."

"You mean, you haven't spoken to your mother since she dismissed you from her house?"

"I've gone by there to apologize but she wasn't in. I've called and all I've gotten was her answering machine. I did, however, apologize on the machine but not in person. All I want is for us to get along and be happy. I'm about to get married and I need my mother. Speaking of mother, I got a call on my answering machine from Brandon's mother. She wants to fly here to help plan my wedding. But as she put it, it's Brandon's wedding, too. Girl, I could have died when I heard that message. I tell you I almost feel like telling Brandon, let's elope."

"Now Linda, you are better than that. All I'm saying is this is your life. Your future mother-in-law will have to take a back seat. This is your wedding. People look at the bride and don't pay much attention to the groom. What I'm saying is, tell Brandon you don't know her, and you would like for him to call her and say you've got everything taken care of."

"But I haven't. And I really don't want to hurt her feelings, but she and I might not like the same things and this is my day not hers. I just don't want to make Brandon pick and choose between his mother and me. I will let him listen to the message and see what he wants to do."

"Okay. What if he wants her to come and help?" asked Denise.

"Then, I'll have to live with her coming to help. I love Brandon and like I said, I don't want him to have to choose. If she comes, I'll call his sister to see if she can come at the same time; then I'll have someone on my side to help me with her."

"Linda, all I can say to you is please, just remember I'm next door, and I have a big mouth and have no problem putting anyone in their place. Especially, when it comes to someone nice like you."

"Thanks Denise, but I don't think I'll need to make that call to you."

We both laughed. I pulled out all the papers so Denise could read all about Paul. I made up my mind that she would be the last person to read them. I had decided that after Denise leaves, I would go outside, and place the entire envelope in the BBQ grill and set fire to it.

"Wow! Girl this man was crazy. Since your mother won't believe you, I think you should mail these papers to her."

"No, I've made up my mind to put this situation in God's hands. I feel that I have faith in God to turn my mother's feelings towards me around. All I've ever wanted was for her to love me. I tell you, only God can do this, and I have faith that he holds the key to doing this."

"Well, I'm going home and let you do what you have to do. I just wanted to hear all about your trip and I'm just so sorry about the relationship between you and your mother. At least you have your father in your life. I just pray that your mother will realize that she's blessed with a wonderful God-fearing daughter. I pray she realizes this before it is too late. Now see me to the door and again; it sure is good having you back home."

Chapter Twenty Three

No sooner had I closed the front door than my mind started retracing the last statement that Denise had made. Paul is dead and I should just leave it be but then what about the young girl? Who will come to her defense? I bet she has told her parents over and over that she was telling the truth about Paul. And I thought about how she would go through the rest of her life being branded a liar. With me holding the truth in the palm of my hands, I had to make the call; I had no choice. If the principal is there, I'll just introduce myself, and let him know that I have some vital information concerning one of his students.

First, I'll ask him to sign a confidentiality statement. The only stipulation is that he would promise not to release the report to the newspaper or media. However, I think he should let the girl's parents and only her parents know that she was telling the truth.

Pacing back and forth, I finally found the courage to make the call.

"Hello, operator, I need the telephone number for New Haven high school, Jacksonville, Florida." She gave me the number and I called the school.

"Hello, my name is Linda Smith, may I speak to the principal, please?"

"Speaking."

"Your name please?"

"Principal Edwards, who is this?"

"I said my name is Linda Smith, and I'm the daughter of Vivian Smith and Paul Richmond."

"Yes, what can I do for you?"

"Sir, I have some helpful information and would like to share it with you. I hired a private detective to gather some information on Paul and I'm willing to share it with you, but only on certain conditions."

"What are the stipulations?"

"That you would sign a confidentiality statement, and that you would not allow the press to read what I am willing to fax to you."

"Young lady, what is this all about? Paul is dead."

"I know, but I feel like the young girl that made the accusation against Paul needs my help. Her name and reputation are at stake here. I want her parents to know that she didn't lie on Paul."

"So you are saying Paul did try something with one of my students? My God, I hired this man! I thought I knew him. What kind of a monster was he?"

"Sir, are you willing to sign the statement and only tell her parents that their daughter was telling the truth?"

"Yes, I promise if you send me the file I'll read it and destroy it immediately. I will type up a statement and fax it to you as you requested."

"Mr. Edwards, I thank you so much and I know this young lady does as well."

I couldn't hang up the phone fast enough. I was finally feeling like by getting this information, the young girl and her family would now have some closure to the situation.

I hung up the phone and was waiting for Brandon to come over, when it rang again.

"Hello."

"Linda, this is Brandon. I have to work late so I won't be coming over this evening."

"That's okay, I understand. By the way, your sister called today."

"What did she have to say?"

"Nothing much, we just talked about the wedding and when she will arrive. Guess who else called? Your mother; she wants to come here to help out with the wedding. If you don't mind, would you please call her and ask her to come in three weeks."

"Why three weeks?"

"Then I can have most of the arrangements in place. See, Brandon, this is our wedding. I wouldn't want to offend your mother or make you chose between us, if we get into an argument."

"Linda, you are right and I'll make the call and ask her to wait a few weeks."

"Thanks."

"Well, I better get back to work," he said. "We can talk tomorrow, okay?"

"Okay, see you later."

Brandon didn't end our conversation with an I love you, so he might be a little angry with me for asking him to call his busybody mother and ask her not to come for a few weeks. I wanted to tell him about my call to Jacksonville, but I didn't feel like this was an appropriate time.

I started my plans into motion immediately. I got out the yellow pages under weddings and started marking off some of the places I planned on calling and visiting tomorrow afternoon. If I could complete my plans in two weeks, before Brandon's mother comes to town, everything will be complete from the flowers at the wedding to the flowers on the table at the reception.

I woke up with a prayer on my heart and wedding plans in my mind. I had written down four different places I was going to call today. I also had to call Melissa. She's the wedding coordinator who attends our church. After I'd viewed some of the pictures in her wedding books, I was confident that she was very capable of doing an excellent job for our wedding.

I rushed to gather my things for work. I knew Marvin had plans to work on the Anderson case. He really didn't trust anyone to work close with him on this case, but me. He kept telling me it was a million-dollar project and he didn't want to lose the bid. I smiled when I thought about it. Here I am a young lady, with such great responsibilities. This just let me know that if God gives you a job to do, he will equip you for the task. That is the kind of God I serve. He stood by me all through college and now here I am about to take another major step in my life. Marriage should not be taken lightly. I'm going to keep God as the head of our family.

My mind began racing again. I better write down Jennifer's name and address. She's one of the soloists in our church choir. That young lady can sing. I mean she's young, but she can hold a tune. I want her to sing the Lord's Prayer, just before my father and I want down the aisle.

Just the thought of my father walking me down the aisle gave me chills. Where will my mother be during all of this? "Lord, please let her gather her thoughts while she's away. Please let her know that I'm not her enemy, but her child, her first born."

All I've ever wanted in life was for my mother to love me. I think that since she gave birth to me at such a young age, I took her youth and somewhere in the back of her mind she blames me. She needs to deal with it and get over it. I'm here now and she is older and supposed to be a Christian lady. She needs to give it a rest. I think, due to Mrs. Carrie and Mr. Mack's teaching, I've turned out to be a very nice, God-fearing, young lady, whom any mother would be proud to call her daughter.

I went from waking up being happy for God allowing me to see another day, to talking about my wedding, to now sad about my mother. I refuse to let Satan win. I have to keep the faith that God holds the key to solving all of my problems. I have to hold on to God's promises. I know that if I walk upright, no good thing He would withhold from me.

I was making my way to the shower when the phone started ringing - again.

"Good morning."

"Good morning, my love."

"Brandon, it sure is good hearing your voice so early in the morning. What's up?"

"Nothing - just wanted to tell my bride to be to have a blessed day. I know you said you had a project you had to work on, and I just wanted to call to let you know that I'm praying for you."

Well, just maybe he isn't a little upset with me for asking him to call his mother after all. I guess this is a good as any time to tell him about me calling the principal of the high school in Jacksonville.

"Brandon, I don't know how to tell you this, but..."

"But what? You can tell me anything."

"Well, I made a call to Jacksonville to speak with the principal."

"You did what?"

"Wait, now let me finish before you comment. I started to think about the poor girl who accused Paul. I felt her family needed some closure. I called and introduced myself to principal Edwards. I told him that I had some helpful information on the Richmond case. I told him this information that I was faxing to him had to be strictly confidential."

"And what did he say after that?"

"He said he would fax me a confidentiality statement to my office. He agreed never to disclose the information I am sending to the media. He would tell the parents that their daughter was telling the truth, and that's all."

"Linda, have you thought this thing through? What if the parents sue your mother?"

"Brandon, my mother doesn't have much, and I am sure they are aware that Paul is dead. I think what's important is that their daughter was telling the truth and they can go on with their lives. I want the girl to be able to hold her head up."

"Okay, if you feel you are doing the right thing then go for it."

"I am. When I get to work I will get his statement then fax some of the paperwork to him."

"Linda, is there anything else you want to tell me concerning Paul?"

"Brandon, I have to get ready for work. We can continue this conversation at a later date. Have a good day."

"You, too, see you later my love," and he hung up.

I rushed to the shower feeling better because I told him about the girl, but now what about telling him what Paul tried to do to me. Should I go into this marriage with this secret hanging over my head? Or shall I tell him? No, not today, I have to wait until the time is right.

No sooner did I get out of the shower, dressed and was headed out the door, when the phone rang again.

"Good morning, Linda."

By the tone of her voice, I knew something was wrong.

"Monica, what a pleasant surprise hearing from you so early this morning."

"Linda, it feels like every time I find time to call you it is because something bad has happened."

"Well, I don't feel that way. Tell me what's up?"

"Eric and I broke up last night," my good friend confided.

"Girl, are you okay?"

"Yeah, I'm alright."

"Has that bruise I saw on your arm got anything to do with the break-up?" I asked. "I didn't want to say anything but I was worried about you."

"Oh, you saw that? Monica murmured."

"Yes, I saw it but it never dawned on me that Eric was the cause of it."

"How long as this been going on?"

"Well, he's only hit me twice."

"Twice! Are you telling me that he's hit you before? And you stayed to let him to do it again?"

"Well, he apologized and swore that he would never do it again. And I loved him enough to believe him. But the look I saw in his eyes last night showed me that it would happen over and over again. I just can't do this so I asked him to leave and not come back."

"Monica, I'm just so sick. I thought Eric was such a great guy. What in the world has brought this on?"

"I don't know, I think it's the stress from the new job. But whatever it was he should have left it there."

"Monica, my stomach turns whenever I think about him hitting you. I just don't understand what would make such a nice man turn abusive."

"This is just a side you have never seen. Eric is a Gemini. It was like he could be one person in the morning and totally different person in the afternoon. I ignored his actions in the past but in the last few months, I've started to question his motives and that is when he started acting up."

"Monica, you are too smart to stand by and take this. Remember what you said about Ralph and Christa's situation. Well, you are in the same situation. Please take your own advice and when he calls don't allow him to come back into your life to play on your emotions."

"Linda, you're right and this time I refuse to take him back. You see, he has done this apologizing before and I usually accept them. He does well for a few weeks then he acts up again. This time I will be strong and leave him forever."

"I'm proud of you and if you feel like you are getting weak, then say a prayer. I read somewhere it said when we are at our weakest, that's when God is at his strongest. He will direct you and give you all the guidance you will need. In other words, ask God to make you strong and not take him back."

"Linda, you aren't the only one who knows God. I, too, pray and have a close relationship with God."

"Monica, I'm not saying you don't know God. I'm just saying for you to pray and ask him to direct your path. I in no way feel like I am the only child of God. I'm just saying to ask him for strength and not take Eric back. Look, I'm sorry I need to get to work. Remember, I love you and so does God."

"I know; I love you, too. And thanks for listening."

"Hey, you're my friend. I'm supposed to listen and most of all I care what happens to you. Now see you later."

I couldn't hang that phone up fast enough. I wanted to scream to the top of my lungs. I was one angry lady. Eric had some nerve putting his hands on her. If she had a brother, you couldn't pay him to put his hands on her. I'm so happy to have Brandon. He is very patient and loving toward me. I pray he doesn't have a second side to him.

Chapter Twenty Four

Two weeks had come and gone; all the wedding plans were set. Brandon and I had finally chosen the perfect invitations. Melissa has been a Godsend. She would meet me each evening to visit the different hotels, and to view their rooms to host my reception. Melissa and I agreed the Hyatt Regency of Atlanta was the perfect place. It was located downtown where everyone could have easy access. Melissa requested that the chef prepare several formal and semi-formal meals. We settled on a formal sit down dinner. Brandon wanted each table to have a glass of champagne with a strawberry in it. I told him that would be very nice for the toast. I asked him what brand of champagne? He replied non-alcoholic, of course.

I was feeling pretty happy seeing that all the wedding plans were now in the works. All I needed now was to hear from my mother. I had made several calls last week and no answer. I didn't want to call Mrs. Williams. I didn't want her to know that my mother and I were still not on good terms. Here it was three weeks before my wedding and no word from my mother. I was happy that my father called about every other day to see if everything was okay. I would tell him everything was shaping up and I would thank him for his concern.

I was feeling good when I walked to the mirror to just take a look at myself. "Mirror, mirror on the wall, I'm the happiest of them all."

Then there was a knock, knock, on the door. "Who in the world is this knocking loudly on my door like the police," I thought.

"I'm coming, just one minute."

There stood Brandon with one of the funniest looking expressions I'd ever seen on his face. "Don't just stand in the elements, come on inside."

Brandon stood aside and this thin, short, gray and white-haired lady was standing behind him. She walked in and extended her hand.

"Hello, I'm Brandon's mother, Mrs. Alexander, but you may call me mother Liz."

I leaned down and looked her straight into her eyes and wanted to say, "I'll call you rude because I told Brandon to tell you to stay in Massachusetts until we call you. And that would have been the day before the wedding."

I smiled, shook her tiny hand and showed her the living room. "Brandon, where is your father?" I asked.

"Dad will be here next week. He thought you and mom would have been a little too busy for him."

"Brandon, didn't you tell your mother that all the plans were now completed?"

"Yes, I tried to tell her, but she insisted on coming," he said.

"Yes, I did and I would like to see the plans. That is if you don't mind, my dear."

"No, not at all. Please have a seat in the living room. Would you care for anything cold to drink?" I offered.

"Yes, what kind of Sherry do you have?"

I wanted to say, "The kind they sell at the neighborhood liquor store, now run down and get some and while you are there, stay and drink it." But I smiled and politely answered, "None. You see, I don't drink."

"Oh, my dear that is so nice of you, but a little red wine is good for the heart."

I wanted to say, "Then you look like you should have a big, healthy, strong beating heart." She looked nothing like I pictured her. I thought she would look well rested, and pretty as a movie star, but no, she looked like she'd had plenty of glasses of wine in her days. The deep circles under her eyes and the heavy makeup didn't help. I wanted to say, "I'm sorry you have missed so much sleep worrying about our wedding. I guess Brandon should have called you earlier."

She settled for a glass of water instead. I wanted so badly to call my neighbor, Denise. She would have put Lady Liz right in her place. But having second thoughts, I didn't need to be making company feel uneasy in my home.

"Tell me, my dear, when will your parents arrive? Surely your mother will be here early, won't she?"

I felt like telling her, first of all my name is Linda, not dear. And my mother's arrival is none of her business. I parted my lips to answer, when I was saved by the telephone.

"Excuse me, I'll get this in the kitchen," I said.

"Hello Linda, this is Lynda, Brandon's sister. Is mother there yet?"

"Why, Lynda, what a pleasant surprise to hear from you, and yes, she has arrived," I reported.

"Isn't she a piece of work? Honey, don't allow mother to make you crazy because she loves to annoy people."

"She hasn't been here that long and already she is making me a little crazy. When are you coming to rescue me?"

"Honey, I know I can't make it for another two weeks, but I will tell you this. I'll call my dad and have him to go there by the end of the week. He is the only one who can take her off of your hands. Brandon will be working and she will be alone. Mother will go stir crazy sitting around watching television all day. I know you are glad to be back to work?"

"You called that one just right. You know I don't feel that she dislikes me, I just get the idea that she wants to be the center of attention."

"Linda, you are one smart lady. That's mother; she likes her attention. All I can say is stick to your plans and do not let her take over. Like it or not, it is your wedding, not Lady Liz's."

We both started laughing - hard. I needed that, but it was back to face reality. I still had the wicked witch sitting in my living room to deal with.

Lynda and I got off the phone. When I went back into the living room, Lady Liz was just entering, too.

"Brandon showed me the condo. Lovely little place you have here. But I do hope when you get married, you will consider selling it and buying a much larger place. How in the world can you host parties in such a tiny place?"

By now I wanted to place both hands around her tiny neck and squeeze until she turned blue. I smiled, took a deep breath and said, "You are right. This is a tiny place, but then I'm the only one who lives here, so it is just right for me."

"Well, my dear, I'm here for you, so if you need me just call. I'll be staying with my son. Come on, Brandon, we have some shopping to do before heading back to your place."

She stood up and headed for the door. I was standing behind her. I felt like balling up my fist and hitting her right in the top of her gray head, but then Brandon was standing in back of me.

"Please come back, and it was nice meeting you. I know we will talk soon," I said as she left.

"You bet, real soon. You said I can look over your wedding plans."

"Oh yes mother Liz, I'll get them together and give them to Brandon. You have a nice evening."

As soon as I shut the door, I felt like screaming, "Please watch your step and I hope a house doesn't fall on you."

I rushed to the telephone to call Denise, but she wasn't home. I was about to explode and I needed someone to talk to. I started mocking how she walked in and her wine conversation. She held out her manicured red nails, with large diamonds on both hands, and diamond bracelets. I know that her husband, Mr. Alexander, is in heaven being home alone.

Brandon got her settled in and called me. He was apologizing all over himself. I had to keep telling him, it was alright, that was his mother acting up, not him. I told him I could deal with her and I wasn't changing our plans for her. I was satisfied with the menu, hotel location, dresses and everything. He assured me that he would handle her and said for me to carry on as if she wasn't even in town. We both said our good nights and that we still loved each other.

No sooner had I hung up the phone that it started to ring again. Please let it be were either Monica or Christa.

"Hello."

"Linda, this is Melissa, how are you?"

"Girl, you wouldn't believe me if I told you. What's up with you?"

"Nothing, I'm just sitting here with nothing to do. Mom is asleep. You know, trying to sleep off yet another drink."

"Hey, Melissa, come on over and we can get the invitations made out, then I can mail them tomorrow."

"Two hundred invitations, wow, are you crazy?"

"Girl, you know I've been working on the labels, so all we have to do is put them on the envelopes," I explained.

"Oh, count me in. I'm on my way. Do you want me to bring a pizza or something?"

"Pizza, with everything on it sounds fine," I said.

"Okay. I'll get the works and also will bring some cokes."

"Come on. I'll pay you for everything," I told her.

"No, I got it this time."

"You'll never guess who's in town?" I exclaimed smugly.

"Who?"

"Brandon's mother."

"Girl, I'm on my way."

I know she will say something about me using these mailing labels. She will say that they don't have that personal touch. Well, Lady Liz isn't writing them, so let's hurry up and get them in the mail.

"Girl, don't let her take your joy. God gave you joy and don't let anyone take it from you," Melissa advised me.

"Melissa, you are right. Hurry up and get here. Thanks."

I was afraid that Brandon's mother was going to ask me about the invitations, so I immediately placed a call to Brandon. I asked his opinion about the labels. He was no help and left the decision up to me. He also reminded me that his list was in my kitchen drawer. I told him since his list only contained about fifty guests, I was going to write out his, so his parents wouldn't see the labels. He said I should stop worrying about something as petty as a label. I needed to take a step back, stop worrying and that the wedding is going to be just beautiful.

Talking to Brandon put me in a much better mood. It was great to know that no matter what, Brandon was in my corner. I got his list from the drawer and started to write out his invitations. I had written about ten when the doorbell rang.

It was Melissa. She had a pizza in both hands and the cokes in a bag sitting on the floor.

"Come on in. I am hungry for food and company," I told her.

"Girl, you sound like me. Now clean off this table so we won't get pizza sauce on your beautiful wedding invitations."

"Especially this one," I said.

"Why is that one so special?"

"Because it belongs to Dr. Olivia Wadsworth," I informed Melissa.

"Who is that?"

"She is the lady who grew up with Brandon and his sister. His sister said they were just friends, but his mother wants her for a daughter-in-law."

"Girl, I'm glad I came over here. Now wait until I fix my plate so we can talk. I want to know the whole story and please don't leave anything out."

"There really isn't anything to talk about. Brandon said they grew up together," I expounded. "His mother loves her because she comes from a family of doctors. They are rich and that is all Brandon's mother cares about: clout, who has money and who hasn't. Well, I don't have the money, but I have Jesus in my life, and that is better than all the money in the world."

Melissa stood up and yelled, "You tell it girl. You may not be a doctor, and you may not be rich, but you are somebody. You are wonderfully made by God."

"Melissa, you're right and when God made me he didn't make no junk. Like you said, I may not be rich with money, but I'm rich when it comes to the word of God."

Melissa and I started laughing. It was really something we both needed since we realized that her mother had the same problem my mother used to have.

"Linda, you said when you went home you found your mother to be a changed lady. What did it take to get her off the bottle?"

"Melissa, it took me and Mrs. Carrie praying – regularly. It also took my mother getting into legal trouble by drinking and driving while under the influence. I tell you it wasn't an easy task, but what I can say is, don't give up on your mother. Keep on praying for her. God will hear your prayers and take the liquor taste from her lips. I once thought my mother would never stop, but God, I tell you God is a keeper of His Word and he is able to take care of it all."

"Linda, it is just so embarrassing to come home and find your mother on the couch drunk."

"Wow, you sound like you have been looking into my past. I know exactly what you mean. I kept on praying and God heard my cry. Like I said, keep on praying for your mother because God is able, and he is a keeper."

"I do pray for her, but I must tell you, she doesn't try to help herself. Sometimes I feel like my prayers are in vain, and that God doesn't even hear me."

"Don't say that. That's how Satan wants you to feel. He wants you to feel defeated, but the word of God says he will never leave you or forsake you. So keep on praying and in his time he will deliver her."

"Linda, you are a witness so I'm going to do just as you say and keep lifting my mother up in prayer. I am glad that I came over. I'm feeling much better already."

"Well, hurry up and eat that pizza so you can lick some labels and envelopes."

We both laughed. It was therapy for us both having her over. She needed my company just as much as I needed hers. It was so good to have Christian friends, with whom to share the word of God.

Chapter Twenty Five

Good morning Holy Spirit, this is the day that the Lord has made. I will rejoice in it. I started to sing the chorus of that song again, because here it was now one week away from my wedding day. Brandon was so comforting to me when it came to me talking about me not hearing from my mother. He kept reassuring me that she would come around, that I needed to have a little faith. I told him that I've put my mother, his mother and all of my problems in the Master's hand. I told him that my faith in God is what held the key to solving all of my problems.

Brandon went to the airport to pick up his sister. She was coming to stay with me so we could do our day spa together. I was so excited that I went through the house twice making sure everything was in order.

Denise came over to inspect my place. She kept me in rare form. She walked in dressed in her red halter jumpsuit.

"Now, don't say a word. I'm only here to inspect your place," Denise commanded. "You know I need to tell you where to place the pillows on the couch and the arrangements on the table."

"No I thought you came here to look around and say you like the new rug I purchased under my coffee table in the living room."

"Oh, I didn't even notice, but it does look good and matches your furniture. You know, Linda, your house always looks good.

"Thanks."

"When does the President and the first Lady arrive?"

"Denise, you should be ashamed of yourself. Brandon would die if he knew you were making fun of his parents. Is this why you are all dressed up to meet them?" I asked.

"No, I'm meeting some friends for a cookout. I could care less what I have on when I meet your future in-laws."

"Denise, you ought to stop. If you keep acting up, I'll never introduce you to the Alexanders."

"I'll probably walk up to them at the wedding, extend my hand and say, hi I'm Denise, your daughter-in-law's neighbor. It's a pleasure meeting you both."

"How would you know Brandon's parents?"

"It will probably be the lady standing in the center of the room looking down her nose at the other guests," mocked Denise.

"Stop it Denise; I hate I told you how she was."

"I'll be on my best behavior I promise to act nice; you can trust me."

Denise said she had things to do. She started walking toward the door. Just before she walked out, she turned to me and said, "Now if the Queen or Lady Liz comes back to hurt you, just call me and I'll come to rescue you."

I told her that won't be necessary because Brandon's at the airport picking up his sister. I told her his sister knew how to handle her mother so I will be in good hands. She went on out the door smiling as if I would still need her help.

Brandon finally pulled up with his sister, Lynda. They were getting out of the car just as I looked out of the window. I rushed to the door to greet her with a hug and kiss.

"Lynda, it is so good seeing you again. Give me a hug and a kiss."

"Girl, you look good, blushing like a bride. I know the feeling. My husband will be here Friday. He had some things to take care of. I told him we would be doing girl things and he would be in the way."

"Lynda, you shouldn't have told him that, but I'm glad you are here early, so we can do the day spa. I also want you to meet my friends and check out the location of the reception."

"Linda, I told you, I'm so happy that Brandon is marrying you and if there is anything I can do, please just ask me."

"Come on inside. I'll show you to your room," I said.

Brandon put her luggage in my guest room while we took a seat in the living room. Lynda was telling me all about how happy she was and that Carlos was a loving husband to her. She was smiling as she talked about him. I found myself blushing at her words.

"So Brandon, where are you taking Linda for your honeymoon?" Lynda inquired of her brother.

"That's a surprise, but I can tell you that we are spending the night at the Hyatt Regency, then will jet off to our four-day honeymoon."

"Brandon, how can you surprise me?" I asked. "I won't know what to pack and how much?'

"Okay, listen the place will be hot, so you will need to pack a bathing suit and something semi-formal for dinner," he relented.

"Dinner... One night dinner, or two?" I snooped.

"Stop it Linda. I'm not telling you where. Listen pack for three days in a hot location and two nights for formal dinner. You may also need to take some nice shorts."

"Sounds like some island to me," guessed Lynda.

"Lynda, hush up. This is between Linda and me," said Brandon.

"Okay, but I'm just as curious and excited for the both of you," relayed Lynda. "Hey, not changing the subject but let's go out for dinner. I'm hungry."

"What do you want?" I asked her.

"Food! Like I said, I'm famished," said Lynda.

"Brandon, are you going by your place to pick up your mother first?" I wondered out loud.

"No, she is spending the day with an old friend who is relocating to Atlanta," he said.

"Good. Let's get out of here before she calls and wants to go with us," said Lynda.

"Sis, you are too hard on mother. She has her way, but then she is a good mother," Brandon said gently.

"Brandon, let's not fight about mother," Lydia said. "You have always been her pick so let's leave her out of it and go to dinner."

We gathered our purses and headed for the door. Brandon did the driving. He was playing tour guide by showing his sister Atlanta. I just sat there thinking about the conversation that they'd had about their mother. I thought, so Brandon is her pet. Then I better do all I can to stay in her good graces. I don't want her to come between us.

Brandon pulled into the Ritz's Steak House. My eyes got as big as golf balls. The last time I'd been to that restaurant was on a date with Brandon. He looked over and smiled at me. I looked into those big beautiful eyes of his and smiled back.

Lynda had to break the silence. "What's all that eye contact about? Am I missing something here?"

"No, this is one of the places I took Linda on a date," explained Brandon to his sister. "The food was wonderful and Linda was so nervous, she dropped her napkin on the floor and was too flustered to ask for another one. The waitress found it next to her and brought her a replacement. Later Linda said she was so embarrassed that she was going to play it off. Linda ordered a steak with red potatoes, and tossed salad with blue cheese dressing."

"Brandon, how in the world do you remember my order?"

"It wasn't hard to remember because every time we have gone out for dinner you order the same kind of salad dressing for your salad," he confided.

"Linda, Brandon is very observant. I bet he could tell you what you wore on your first date," Lynda surmised.

"Stop it, Lynda, I'm not that bad. The first date I spent my time looking into her eyes," he said. "She has the most beautiful eyes and I think that is what attracted me to Linda in the first place."

"Brandon stop it, you are making me blush," I admitted.

"You should be blushing because I love you, girl."

"Wait until I get out of this car and get me something to eat," said Lynda. "All of this love stuff is making me miss Carlos, and I just saw him a few hours ago."

When we got inside the restaurant it seemed crowded but the hostess recognized Brandon immediately. I wanted to ask him if he came here often, but I didn't want to put a damper on dinner.

Brandon must have read my facial expression because the moment we were seated, he started to explain that he and a few of the doctors had lunch at this location twice in the last two weeks. I smiled with a sigh of relief. I was looking at the hostess as she left the table and noticed how pretty and well proportioned she was. I found myself getting a little jealous.

The waiter came to the table with a pleasant demeanor. He was very excited about the specials, but I knew I only wanted a well done steak, red potatoes, and cole slaw. I was smiling at him because he was in such an upbeat mood. It was refreshing to see someone happy with his job. Lynda ordered a medium well steak, baked potato with butter only, and a garden salad with ranch dressing. Before the waitress could look at me for my order, Lynda asked for a glass of white wine. However, then she looked at Brandon and me and said to the waiter "never mind, I'll take iced tea."

Brandon ordered a steak, half slab of ribs, baked potato with butter and sour cream, and a garden salad with French dressing.

"Sis, do you want the wine or not? He asked Lynda. "Don't feel badly because Linda and I don't care for any."

"It's not that. I forgot. I think I'm going to have a little one," she said.

"You mean I'm going to be an uncle?'

"Yes, and Linda you will be an aunt."

Brandon reached over and squeezed her hand. I leaned over and gave her a big hug.

"So you see, my wine and champagne days are over," Lynda said.

"Have you told mom and dad yet?" asked Brandon.

"Are you crazy? I'm going to make sure I'm expecting before I spring the news on Lady Liz," said

Lynda. "I know she would be happy, but you know she doesn't like to be disappointed, so I better be very sure before telling her."

"You're right, but I'm sure she will be happy and would make a good grandmother," he said.

"Yes, after she gets over the shock of not being the center of attention anymore," Lynda retorted.

They both shared in the laughter at their mother's expense.

The food arrived and not a minute too soon. Lynda had already made reference to the fact that she was starving and the iced tea wasn't filling her up.

Brandon said the grace, while Lynda and I bowed our heads. I wanted to thank God for just this moment, but when I looked up Lynda had a mouth full of salad.

We all commented about how well our food tasted. Lynda kept saying her steak was a little too well done for her. Brandon urged her to have it taken back so they could prepare one to her liking, but she refused to give it up. She said she was too hungry to wait for another one.

After dinner, Brandon wanted to do some walking downtown, but Lynda said she was a little tired, so we went back to my house for dessert. I had taken a frozen coconut cream pie out to thaw. Lynda was all for that. She kept saying how she always had room for a good dessert.

Entering the house, I noticed the blinking light on my answering machine. I pushed the button all the while hoping it was a message from my mother.

"Brandon, I mean Linda, hi, this is mother Liz. If Brandon and Lynda are there, please tell either one to call me. Especially Lynda; she's got some nerve coming into town and not calling me. Thanks."

"Wow! You both heard the message. Now which one of you is going to call her first?"

"Not me. I want to eat my dessert in peace," said Lynda. Brandon, she's at your house and if you don't want to face a bear the moment you hit the door, I suggest you call her now."

"Lynda, not tonight," he said. "I'll deal with her when I get home. Anyway, she will probably be asleep. I have to pick up dad tomorrow from the airport. Hey, do either one of you want to ride with me?"

"What time is dad's flight?" asked Lynda.

"He said he should arrive about nine in the morning."

"I'll pass," Lynda said. "You take mom with you."

"Oh, she is definitely riding. I just wanted to see if either one of you wanted to go along."

"Brandon, since Lynda isn't going, then I'll stay here with her. I know, why don't we meet you guys downtown for a light lunch."

"Okay with me, how about you, sis?"

"You know I'm available and it will be great seeing dad again," Lynda said.

"What about mom?" Brandon smirked.

"Brandon, go home, Linda and I are tired of you so go home. We will see you tomorrow about noon."

"Speak for yourself. I'm never tired of such a handsome man as this," I intoned.

"Oh my goodness, you got the rest of your life to be with Brandon," Lynda responded. "Go on home so Linda and I can spend some time together. See you tomorrow."

I walked Brandon to the front door. He lightly kissed me on the lips and headed to his car. I started thinking I sure do hope his mother is asleep. Brandon is in such a good mood and I would hate for her to upset him, just days before our wedding.

Lynda was on the phone talking to Carlos when I came back into the living room. She was blushing and smiling. I waved good night and headed for my shower.

After my long, hot shower, I walked back into the dark living room. Lynda had turned off all of the lights and it was even dark in her room. I quietly made a cup of tea and took it back to my room.

I sat in the chair, took out my Bible to have a little quiet time with the Lord. I opened my Bible to Psalm 91: *He that dwelleth in the secret place of the most High shall abide under the shadow of the Almighty.* My mind started to reflect back on Mrs. Carrie. She was such a wise, God-fearing lady. I know that if she was still here, she would tell me something like, "Linda, in a few days one chapter of your life will end, but another one begins. If you and Brandon keep God as the head of your marriage nothing will come up against you that the three of you can't handle."

I smiled to myself thinking about her. I thank God for placing her in my life. I stood up, closed the Bible and walked over to my closet. I reached to the very top to locate a box of scarves. If my memory served me right, I thought Mrs. Carrie had a nice lace blue one. I looked and finally came upon it. I made up my mind that I was going to be holding that in my right hand under my flowers, as I walked down the aisle. I needed something blue and this will be special because it belonged to Mrs. Carrie. Having a piece of Mrs. Carrie will make me feel like she is there with me.

I took the scarf and placed it under my nose. I could still smell her perfume. I closed my eyes and could actually see her smiling face in my mind. I opened my eyes and the tears started to flow down my face. God I miss her so much, and with my mother acting like she is all I could do is cry and lean back on the chair.

After my good cry, I dried my eyes, put the scarf back into the box, and placed the box back on the shelf.

I got down on my knees for a word of prayer. "Dear Heavenly Father, I thank you for this day. Lord you have been so good to me. Lord I need your anointing on me; please let my mother know that she still has me in her life. Please let her call me or show up to my wedding. Lord this would be all I need. I thank you for allowing me to find my father and for letting him love me and wanting to share his life with me. Now Lord, I also ask for you to please be in the midst of my marriage. Please soften Brandon mother's heart, so she may receive me as her daughter-in-law. Lord, I thank you in advance for making all my prayers come true."

Chapter Twenty Six

Bacon, eggs, grits, or potatoes, all I can say is something is smelling good in this house. I rushed to the kitchen to find my future sister-in-law Lynda with my favorite apron around her waist cooking away.

"Good morning, Lynda."

"Linda, I hope I didn't disturb you?"

"No, it was time for me to get up, but the odor is what did the trick. What are you cooking?"

"I thought I would surprise you with some hash brown potatoes, sausage, and eggs," she responded.

"You're supposed to be my guest and let me do the breakfast, but I thank you for going to all this trouble."

"No trouble at all, you go on and get freshened up while I finish."

I did as she suggested. Looking at the portions she was serving up, it sure was a lot of food for just the two of us.

I went on to make up my bed then lay out my nice navy blue, short-sleeved, silk suit. I wanted to look nice when I met Brandon's father for the first time.

I came back to the kitchen to find the table all setup for three. I looked in the living room and to my surprise sat mother Liz.

"Good morning, dear. Brandon dropped me off to share breakfast with you two. I told him this was a wonderful idea."

"Yes, it was," I said trying not to show I was surprised by her presence.

"You both better come to the table while it is good and hot," Lynda exhorted. "I want you to know that I really don't do this often but this is a special occasion. Not every day do I get to be with my mother and sister-in-law."

I smiled and so did mother Liz. Lynda said the grace and we passed the serving plates. Lynda had really outdone herself. The food was tasty and the eggs were light and fluffy.

Lynda revealed that her husband Carlos' flight would get in Friday at nine. "He said he knew that we girls wanted to have some fun, so he thought Friday would be a better day," she said.

"It will because Monica and Christa will be here Thursday morning," I said. "Some of my friends and co-workers are giving me a bridal shower. It will be held at my job in one of the nice large conference rooms."

"What time is the shower?" Lynda asked.

"It's not until 6 o'clock that evening. That would give people time to clear out for the day and that would give them plenty of time to decorate the room."

"They must think a lot of you to have it at your job," mentioned Lynda.

"They are some wonderful ladies to work with, plus the location is great," I responded.

I cleared the table and left Lynda and her mother talking over coffee. I started the dishwasher when the phone rang.

"Hello."

"Hello Linda, this is Brandon. Please tell mom that dad's flight will be two hours late, so we will have to call lunch off and do dinner."

"Good because your sister made an awesome breakfast and we are too full for lunch in a few hours. Maybe we will go to the mall for a little shopping."

"Okay, I'll see you about four."

"That was Brandon, he said to tell you both that his father's flight is going to be two hours late, so instead of lunch we will meet for an early dinner. He will call us about four."

"Well my dear, come back to the table so we may discuss your wedding plans," beckoned mother Liz. "I looked them over and found them to be excellent."

I almost lost my tongue. Did I hear her say she thought the plans were excellent? Now, I know Brandon must have had a little talking to her, but thank God for small favors.

"Linda, lets hit the shopping center. I want to buy your bridal shower gift," said Lynda.

"Me, too," her mother added.

I went into the candle shop while mother Liz and Lynda went into Victoria Secret to do a little shopping. We met in the middle of the mall. They both were smiling with their pink bags in hand. I wanted to ask is all that for me, but I knew it probably was.

We looked at our watches and it was ten minutes to four. We went back into the candle shop, so I could call Brandon. He was at his place with his father waiting on our call.

"Linda, where are you girls?"

"Don't kill us; we are still at the mall. What is your father doing?" I asked politely.

"He is sitting in my living room waiting for dinner. He only ate some peanut butter crackers; he didn't want to spoil his dinner."

"Since we are at the mall, would you and your father want to meet us at the Steak n Lobster restaurant?"

"Good idea, you all go and make reservations for six. Dad and I will be there in fifteen minutes."

"Six, Brandon you mean five don't you?"

"No, I have a wonderful surprise for you. Now don't say another word. See you soon."

No sooner than I hung up the phone that mother Liz was almost in my face. She wanted to know if her husband got in and when will she see him. I told her the plans are for them to meet us at the mall.

We walked over to the restaurant. It had a nice, long line out front. I told them this place has great food and it was worth standing in line for. Mother Liz didn't care for that, so she walked on a few doors down to the shoe store to do more shopping.

Lynda and I made the reservation. We sat and watched the people as they walked by. Lynda stood up and started waving at Brandon and this tall handsome man. "Dad, you look good, now come here and give me a hug," she said.

"Lynda you look good, too. Now this must be Linda. You are as pretty as Brandon says," his dad complimented.

I was blushing and shaking his hand at the same time. Mother Liz must have heard us talking because we looked up and she was rushing toward us.

"Baby, you made it. Isn't Linda such a beautiful girl?
I tell you I'm just so proud of Brandon."

I wanted to say, you've got to be kidding. What about your precious Olivia? I think Brandon must have had a talk with her. She was now sweeter than syrup to me.

A little short gray-headed lady walked briskly toward us. She was smiling and so was everyone else, except me. I was the only one looking puzzled when she ran into Lynda's waiting arm.

"Grandma, how are you?" greeted Lynda.

"Honey, it is good seeing you again, now let me get some sugar from this pretty young lady."

She reached and hugged and kissed me. It was like being in the presence of Mrs. Carrie again. She wore her hair parted down the middle and flipped under. I was smiling and crying on the inside. She had large friendly eyes like Mrs. Carrie, too. All I could do was hold her tight and smile.

"Grandma, this is Linda," said Brandon.

"I know she is as pretty as you said she would be. My name is Mary Louise Alexander, but you may call me Grandma."

"Grandma, it is a pleasure meeting you," I said.

Our table was called and we all went into the restaurant for a family dinner. Brandon's father did most of the talking while we all listened. He was a man of charm and wisdom. He reminded me of someone who had traveled the world and lived an interesting life. I found myself hanging on to every word that came out of his mouth.

Mother Liz was on her best behavior, which made the dinner pleasant. I was listening and watching how lady like she was conducting herself. All the while I was thanking God for making this day and allowing me to be a part of such a wonderful family.

I often found myself taking a glance at grandmother. I couldn't get it out of my mind how much she reminded me of Mrs. Carrie, especially, when she gave the grace. I closed my eyes and I thought I actually heard the voice of Mrs. Carrie, but when I opened my eyes it was Brandon's grandmother.

Grandmother would look in my direction and flash a warm and friendly smile and I would find myself doing the same back to her.

Lynda broke her silence by saying she can't wait until Carlos comes to town. She missed him something terrible. Brandon told her he now knows how it feels to be in love. He stood up and said for all of us to hold up our glasses, he wanted to make a toast.

"I just want to say, first of all, I'm so happy you all are here with Linda and me," Brandon declared. "I also want to thank God for placing such a wonderful lady in my life. I know if we keep God in our lives we will have a successful marriage. Now let's toast to happiness."

We all clicked our glasses together and said happiness in unison. Brandon's grandmother stood and said, "Now, because I am the oldest at this table everybody has to listen to me for a minute. I watched Lynda and Brandon grow up, and I must say your parents did a real good job with you both. I'm so proud to be your grandmother. Brandon, I know you will make a good husband to Linda and if he acts up, just call me." Everyone started laughing. We continued to eat our dinner and talked late into the evening.

Chapter Twenty Seven

Good morning Holy Spirit. It is Thursday. I better get myself up and make it to the airport to pick up Monica and Christa. I have so much to do today. I walked into the living room to find Lynda dressed in her black pantsuit. She was drinking a cup of coffee.

"You mean no breakfast?" I asked.

"I had some cold cereal, so I wouldn't be starving. I knew you had to pick up your friends and I figured if you're hungry, I could do the driving and could drive you to McDonald's for a sausage and biscuit," suggested Lynda.

"I'm a little too excited for breakfast, but thanks."

"After we pick up the girls, I will treat the four of us to a pampering session at the day spa," Lynda said.

"I know Monica and Christa would love that. I can pay half of the bill," I offered.

"No, this is my treat."

"Thanks."

"I do have a suggestion. After the pampering session, let's head over to the Underground for a good seafood meal," said Lynda.

"I'm all for that. I should be ready to eat by then."

We arrived at the airport just as Monica and Christa were coming out of the door from the ramp. They both were smiling and screaming, as if, they hadn't seemed me in ages. I parked the car and ran into their arms. They both looked great. They had luggage enough to stay for a week instead of a few days. I told them our plans were to go to Essentials for a massage then off to the Underground for lunch. They were happy about anything just as long as it made me happy.

"Lynda, these are my two best friends, Monica and Christa."

"Hello, it is a pleasure meeting you both. I want you to know that I'm one lucky sister-in-law to have Linda. I know she is going to make my brother a great wife."

"Thanks and I promise if you are pregnant, then I plan on being a great aunt too," I said.

Monica asked Lynda when her baby was due. Lynda told her she needed to see the doctor when she returned home to confirm that she is expecting.

The ride to Essentials Day Spa was full of girl talk. Lynda started talking about Carlos and Christa talking about Ralph. Monica was just listening. As I watched Monica's expressions through the rear view mirror, I could see how sad she was. I know she hates the fact that she and Eric were no longer a couple, but I know she was doing the right thing in letting him go before he physically hurt her.

We pulled into the parking lot, when Lynda turned around to tell Monica and Christa that they would love what they were about to experience. She told them since she didn't know if she was expecting, she would just get her nails manicured.

We walked in and the receptionist remembered me and asked us to please be seated. Monica and Christa were so impressed with the place. I told them wait until they get the full treatment.

Megan and Tara walked in with smiles on their faces. They were so happy to see Lynda and me. Lynda told them she wasn't getting a massage only a manicure. Megan called for Tamara to come out. She walked in looking like she just stepped out of a magazine. Her blond hair was cut short and worn close to her head. She had a little makeup on and it was flawless. Her thick lips were covered with light red lipstick. What made her simply beautiful were her green eyes, and long eyelashes. She extended her hand and introduced herself to all of us.

Monica, Christa and I followed Megan, Tara and Tamara to the dressing room. Monica and Christa were looking as we were walking through the salon. When we were given our plush robes that did it. Monica was the first to say how soft and white they were. Christa said ditto to all the comments that were made my Monica.

The three of us were given our pedicure first, then the manicure next. When it was time for our massages, we were taken to individual rooms.

One hour later, we all met back in the dressing room. Monica and Christa said this was their first time at a day spa but I could be sure it wouldn't be their last. I had to confess to them that my future sister-in-law introduced me to this place and I have promised to make it a part of my life.

Lynda was seated in the receptionist area patiently waiting. Her nails were French polished and she was sipping on a glass of bottled water.

"Lynda, I can't thank you enough for the wonderful day at the spa," said Monica.

"Monica, you are more than welcome."

"Lynda, I must say this was my first massage, but it won't be my last one. I thank you so much for introducing me to a new way of pampering myself," added Christa.

"Christa, you are more than welcome."

We all were hungry and thirsty, so we rushed off to Atlanta's Underground mall for a well-deserved meal. I told them in the car to order anything on the menu, that I was doing the treating. Christa was the first to say she was hungry and she was going to order big and eat it all. Monica reminded her that she still had to fit in her bridesmaid dress, so she better not eat too much. Her comment was she would leave off the dessert. Lynda was laughing and talking as if we had all know each other forever.

Lunch was tasty and filling. Now all we wanted to do was rush across town to my condo. They had to unpack and get ready for my bridal shower at 6. Brandon's friends were taking him out for what they called his last night of being single. I told him to have fun and just be careful.

We arrived at my condo and were greeted by Denise, my neighbor. She wanted to meet my two friends before the shower.

"Hello, my name is Denise and I'm Linda's neighbor."

Introductions were made and then Denise followed us into the condo. I showed the girls their rooms while I came back into the living room to entertain Denise. She went into the kitchen to get herself a bottle of water while I took a much needed seat. I found myself tired and just felt like a short nap would make all the difference. Denise wanted to know all about my day and I gave her details on the day at the spa and lunch afterwards. She noticed the girls never came out, but I told her they were probably getting unpacked and then probably will lie down for a few hours before the shower. She understood and got up to leave.

"Linda, I'll see you in a few hours at the shower, now don't be late," said Denise.

"No, I won't be late and I will see you there."

I walked back to the bedrooms to find all three of the girls in their beds fast asleep. I went back into the living room to lie down for a few hours of rest.

The phone starting ringing off the hook, and as I reached for it I was wondering who in the world is disturbing my rest.

I said, "Hello."

"Linda, this is Denise, you better get up and get ready for your shower."

"What time is it?"

"It's 4 o'clock and your shower is in two hours."

"Girl, we all are knocked out over here. I guess the massages just relaxed us so we all went to sleep."

"Well, you better get up. Ain't nothing like being late at your own shower."

"Denise, you are a good friend and a great neighbor."

"Yeah, yeah, you better get on up."

"I will and thanks, see you there."

"Bye."

"Bye."

I woke the girls and we all rushed around the condo getting our showers and getting dressed for the bridal shower. I was the first one to be dressed and was sitting in the living room waiting.

Monica, Christa, and Lynda finally came in. They had their neatly wrapped gifts and were ready to head out.

"Girls before we leave here I want a group hug, and I want to say that I love all three of you and I'm just so happy you all are here with me."

"Now don't start crying, I don't feel like washing my face and reapplying my make up," said Christa.

"Oh, hush up Christa and get out of here," I said.

"Monica, are you crying?" I asked; now don't you start."

"I'm not crying, I just have something in my eye."

"Yes, love for me," I said.

"Go on Linda and let's get out of here, we have a shower to attend," said Monica.

The bridal shower was fun; seemed like the entire company came to support me. They went all out for the affair. The food was great, and the gifts, my God I had to get Mary to follow me home in her jeep to bring some of the larger gifts. Brandon's mother seemed to enjoy herself. Maybe it was because Benny, who likes to drink imported wine, kept taking her near his desk. I'm sure he was giving her a few glasses because all the way home she kept saying how much she enjoyed the shower.

We drove mother Liz and grandma to Brandon's house, but it was hard getting mother Liz out the car. She kept saying she waned to hang out with us girls. Brandon's father, Mr. Alexander, got her into the house and we drove off. Lynda apologized for her mother's action, and said she doesn't live with them so she couldn't say why her mother all of a sudden has taken up drinking wine. We told her she had nothing to apologize for.

We got to my condo and all got situated. I gave Christa my other guest room and told Monica we could share my big queen size bed. I sat in the living room going through all of the gifts I had received. Lynda was on the phone with Carlos making sure we were still to pick him up at the airport in the morning.

We girls spent most of the evening sitting around the dining room table talking about life. Lynda, being the oldest had plenty to school us on. It was starting to get late when Lynda was the first to say her goodnight. I was the last one to leave the table, so I turned off the lights and headed to the bedroom.

Carlos had an early flight, so Lynda and I left Monica and Christa asleep. We decided to leave early since I lived quite a way from the airport. When we got halfway there the traffic started to pick up. I could see Lynda was getting a little nervous. I wanted to say we will arrive soon, but all I did was to make comments about the heavy traffic and drove on.

We finally arrived at the airport, but there was still a little distance to the Delta sign. As I drove closer, I could see Lynda looking trying to locate her husband. Finally, we were two signs from Delta, when Lynda located Carlos. He was standing right under the Delta passenger pickup sign.

"Carlos, that's him, the handsome man standing under the Delta sign."

"You mean the good looking man in the all black two piece suit?"

"You got it, that's Carlos."

I pulled to the curb when Lynda jumped out and into his waiting arms. I found myself smiling and so happy to see two people so much in love. She stated speaking in Spanish and he was talking back in his native language.

I popped the trunk so he could place his luggage in and watched him walk her back to the front of the car.

"Carlos, this is Linda, Linda this is Carlos."

"Please to meet you," He said.

"Please to meet you too," I agreed.

Lynda was talking a mile a minute all the way back to the condo. I stopped for some takeout so the girls could have some brunch, because I figured Carlos was hungry too.

We spent the day sitting around the house, while Brandon did a lot of last minute running around. My dad called. He wanted directions to my condo and the church. He told me that he was staying in a hotel across the street from the Hyatt. He had brought a nurse with his mother. I was happy that he made it, but sad because here I was getting married tomorrow and not even a word from my mother.

We all met at church at 5 o'clock for the wedding rehearsal, which went as planned. Everyone was there except my mother. I tried to keep smiling but inside my heart was crushed. If my mother was dead I could accept that, but tomorrow will be My Day and she will be a no show. I held back the tears as my father and I walked down the aisle. When we got to the part of the program where Mary sings the Lord's Prayer, the tears began running out of my eyes. I just couldn't suppress them any longer.

The church got quiet. Brandon pulled me aside and tried to get me to hold on. He reminded me of what I'd said about *faith holding the key*. I lightly smiled and told him all I have now is my faith and you. He then asked me if God had ever let me down. I looked at him like he was nuts. I told him no way, I serve an on time God. Then he told me to have faith in Him. I wiped my tears and we went through the rehearsal again.

My father introduced me to my grandmother's nurse. She was a nice middle-age lady. I watched how she had so much patience with my grandmother. She said it was a pleasure being there and for me not to worry about a thing. She would take care of my grandmother.

Dad took the entire wedding party to dinner. He was staying at the hotel across from the Hyatt because he had paid for a private dinner to be served in the dining room there. Grandmother looked so pretty and she was all smiles every time she would look in my direction.

"Grandmother, I'm so very happy you are here with me."

"Linda, I wouldn't have missed it for the world. I made a promise to God, that if he allowed me to travel I would be here to support you on your special day."

I leaned down and kissed her on the cheek. I wanted to say, here you are in a wheelchair and yet didn't let your health keep you away. Mom is just being selfish, but I have to have faith that she will make it in the morning.

Everyone said their good-byes and went their separate ways. I told Brandon I needed him to come to the condo; that we needed to have a talk. He kissed me on the forehead and followed me in his car.

When we arrived, we walked hand-in-hand around to the back of my condo to sit on the deck so we could talk in peace.

Brandon sat in one chair and I sat in the other facing him. He gently held my hands and looked seriously into my eyes. I gently took my hands from his and said to him.

"Brandon, I want you to just listen to what I have to say before you make any kind of comment."

"Linda, you are frightening me."

"No need to be frightened. I just need to go into this marriage with a clear conscience. What I'm saying is, remember the first trip I made to Jacksonville? The one where I was in a terrible accident and was laid up in the hospital in a coma?"

"Yes, I remember."

"Well, mother wasn't home. She was on her way to the airport to pick you up. I was supposed to be dressed, but I decided to take a quick shower, when Paul picked the lock rushed into the bathroom and tried to rape me."

Brandon stood up, threw his hands up in the air and said, "Linda, I knew he tried something because of your action towards him. And when you were adamant about hiring a private investigator, it just didn't sit too well with me."

"Brandon, please come back and sit. Please don't hate me. I wanted to tell you from the beginning, but I didn't want to hurt you or my mother. Please forgive me for this burden I've been carrying around until now. I didn't want to marry you with this hanging over my head. And if you don't want to still marry me, I'll understand."

"Linda, are you crazy? I love you more than life itself and I knew in my heart something was up. I'm just as much to blame as you. I should have pressured you into telling me, but I thought if my theory was true you would come to me first. Come here and let me hold you in my arms. I want you to know that I will never let anything like this happen to you again. I promise to love and protect you."

Emotions were flying high; we both we crying. I was crying because he still wanted to marry me. I think he was crying because of me almost being hurt by Paul. All I know is that I'm happy this was behind me and we could go on with our lives as husband and wife beginning the next day.

Good morning Holy Spirit, this is the day that the Lord has made. The sun is shining bright and I'm ready to become Mrs. Brandon Alexander. I went into the living room to find everyone eating and talking. Brandon's father had gone for takeout so no one had to worry about being hungry during the wedding. I thanked him for being so thoughtful.

The phone rang and it was Brandon. He explained that he was sorry about not making it to breakfast, but he wanted to wait and see me coming down the aisle of the church. He reminded me that would be in three hours and for me not to be late. He reassured me that he still loved me and that what we talked about last night was placed in the sea of forgetfulness.

His grandmother saw the expression on my face after I hung up the phone. She came to where I was sitting and said, "Honey, you love my grandson and I know you will be a good wife. I'm so proud that Brandon waited for God to bless him with a great girl like you."

"Grandmother, thank you."

Brandon's parents came over where grandmother and I were talking. They had a surprise for me.

"Linda, Liz and I want you to know that we are so proud of you and wish you all the happiness with Brandon. We have a personal gift for you; please consider it as something new."

Mother Liz pulled this neatly wrapped box out of her purse and gave it to me. She sealed it with a hug and a kiss. Brandon's father did the same. I slowly removed the bow, as my fingers were nervously shaking. I was finally able to get the paper off. I carefully opened the box and couldn't believe my eyes. They had given me the most beautiful pair of diamond earrings. Everyone came over to get a closer look.

"Way to go Linda, those are big and beautiful," said Monica.

"Thanks, Monica, they sure are."

"Only the best for our daughter-in-law," said mother Liz.

"Thanks, mother Liz."

"Okay everyone, Melissa said for me to be on time, so let's head off to the church."

I wanted to be there early so I could look in the church to see how the decorations looked. I knew Melissa hired the best, because I had to write the big check.

Denise was a good friend as well as neighbor. She followed us to the church with Monica and Christa in her car. She told them she was their transportation to the airport when it was time to go. I thanked her because I was going straight to my honeymoon.

We arrived at the church just as people were starting to come in. I was looking in to see who all made it from Jacksonville. Melissa asked me what I thought about the decorations? I told her they were beautiful and the live roses in purple and white were just elegant.

I saw some familiar faces from my home church in Jacksonville. I noticed Mrs. Williams sitting with Mrs.

Evyonne, but I wasn't about to let them know I was peeping.

As I turned to make my way down the hall to my separate room to get dressed, I ran right into the path of Mrs. Love.

"Mrs. Love, you made it! Oh, thank you."

"Honey, an entire bus of us came from Jacksonville. No way we were going to let our Linda get married without being there."

"I saw Mrs. Williams and Mrs. Evyonne."

"Well, when you make it down that aisle you will see a lot more," Mrs. Love said. "Now go on and get dressed and be happy. God let the sun shine beautifully for you today, now you shine for him."

"Thank you I will."

I went into a separate room from the wedding party to get dressed. But just as I was about to close the door, my grandmother was wheeled in. She gave me a long gray box. Inside was a single sting of pearls.

"Honey these were worn by me at my wedding. They were given to me by my dear mother, and now I'm passing them to you," said grandmother.

I leaned down and gave her a big kiss.

"Thanks, now I have something old, something new, and something blue."

Lynda pushed the door opened and said, "Excuse me, but I was listening to you say you had something old, something new, and something blue. Well, here is my diamond bracelet. And now you have something borrowed. And I want it back before the honeymoon."

Grandmother got a big laugh at what Lynda said about me returning her bracelet. Her nurse thought it was funny, too. I kissed my grandmother on the cheek and thanked her again. Her nurse said she had to wheel her out, so I could get dressed. Melissa patiently waited for me. She had all of my things laid out all I had to do was to step in the dress, while she buttoned me up.

"Linda, this dress is beautiful. You are going to make such a beautiful bride. I mean, when those doors open and Brandon sees you walking down the aisle, all I can say is wow! You look beautiful."

"Thanks Melissa, you have helped to make my day simply beautiful and if I haven't told you, I'm so grateful for all the help you have given me."

Melissa grinned and said, "Now come over here and sit so I can place your veil on your head."

"Melissa, before you do that please give me a few minutes to myself. I want to walk over to that chair where my lock box is. I need to spend some time with God."

"I'll go and check on the others. I'll be right back, so take your time with the Lord."

"Thanks."

She left the room. I sat down and took my Bible and note pad out of my locked box. I said to my heavenly father, "Lord you have been so good to me and I just want to take the time to thank you for everything. I don't understand why my mother didn't come, but you do. I'm going to take my pen and mark off everything on my list because you have answered my prayers. I still have faith that she will walk through that door."

I took my pen and marked out all of my problems and considered them solved. I closed the Bible and turned around and through my tears I actually thought I saw the shadow of my mother standing in the doorway looking at me. I wiped my eyes and clearly saw it was my mother standing in the doorway.

"Mother, how long have you been standing there?" I exclaimed.

"Long enough to hear your prayer."

I started in her direction when she met me halfway and said, "Linda, I'm so sorry it took me this long to come to my senses. I've been to counseling and I recently spoke to Brandon. He convinced me that you needed me. I'm so ashamed of all the troubles I've caused you in life, please forgive me."

"Mother, don't say another word. God has taken care of all of my problems and He has answered my prayers. I knew in my heart that He was the key and I had faith in him."

While embracing each other, my father walked into the room to say it was time. He looked at my mother. She looked at him.

"Vivian, my God, it's you."

"Yes, Alphonso, it's me."

We motioned for him to come and join in our family circle. He swiftly joined our waiting arms. The three of us hugged and cried together; they were tears of joy. I said in my spirit, I'm so happy. I finally got what I've always wanted in my life: a mother to show me love and a father who loves me unconditionally. In my spirit, I was thanking God for this very moment. I knew my faith in God is what held the key to solving all of my problems.

About The Author

Francine A. Yates lives in Indianapolis, Indiana with her husband Benjamin, and two children, Donald and Patrice. She attended Indiana University-Purdue University in Indianapolis.

Fran has been a mentor at an Indianapolis public school. She created a book club at the Wheelers Boys & Girls Club of Indianapolis.

Fran's active memberships include: Pleasant Union Missionary Baptist Church, Church Women United, and Authors Supporting Authors Positively (ASAP).

To schedule Book Signings or Speaking Engagements Contact:

Francine A. Yates
P.O. Box 18982
Indianapolis, IN 46218
Fran3214@yahoo.com
www.franyates.net

www.ingramcontent.com/pod-product-compliance
Lightning Source LLC
La Vergne TN
LVHW050615100826
845148LV00011B/1598
9780977852116